Highway To Heck
A Select Your Own Timeline Adventure

CHUCK TINGLE

DEDICATION

To all the buckaroos who keep on truckin' for love.

HOW TO READ THIS BOOK:

Welcome to The Tingleverse, a place where unicorns, bigfeet, dinosaurs and living objects are a typical part of our daily lives. This reality is similar to the one that you're currently reading from, but positioned on a slightly different timeline.

Every action you take, or don't take, creates several new timelines of reality. These worlds have been blossoming into existence since the universe began, and will continue until it ends. It's a power that we all have, but rarely know we're using.

This book will illustrate just how important making choices can be. Unlike most books, which are read chronologically from front to back, you read a Select Your Own Timeline book by following the instructions in italics at the bottom of most pages. If there is only one option, these words will inform you which page to turn to next. However, there will often be multiple choices that you, the reader, get to select on this important journey.

These forks in your journey will look similar to this:

To order the spaghetti, turn to page 1325
To order the chocolate milk, turn to page 7489
Leave the restaurant on page 3244

If there are no words in italics at the bottom of your page (or story ending), it is assumed you should continue reading onto the next chronological page of the book, as you normally would.

Throughout your Tingleverse journey, you will sometimes find an item that you can carry with you. It's important to remember the items you've collected, so using a piece of scrap paper to write them down as you go might be helpful, though not required. When you receive an item, it will be written in all capital letters LIKE THIS.

The only other time you will see something written plainly in all capital letters is if you reach the end of a particular timeline path, and thusly the end of your story. It will be written as THE END.

If you come to a path that explicitly involves an item you don't have, you cannot take this path. If you cannot remember whether or not you possess an item, then it's assumed you do not. In this case you lost your item or left it somewhere along your journey.

Sometimes, a specific path you take will cause you to lose an item. If an item is lost, it will be written in all capitals and italics, *LIKE THIS*. Sometimes, instead a specific item, you will lose *ANY ITEMS* you are carrying.

If you ever return to the first page, you will automatically lose all of your items.

Now that we've covered all the rules, please enjoy your journey through the various timelines of The Tingleverse! Your tale begins on page one.

It's been a long road to get here, both literally and figuratively. During your stint journeying as a big-rig truck driver across the wide open American landscape, you've seen all kinds of things and had plenty of adventures, but now it's finally time to call it a day.

You've put in your hours and worked as hard as you could, spent grueling nights trying to make it over a snowy mountain pass or long days in the sun as you powered through the desert with a broken air conditioner and nothing more than a tape deck to keep you company.

After all this, there's a powerful feeling that comes over you as you stroll into the warehouse for your last assignment: pride.

Who knows what's next for you, whether you plan on jumping in with another job or simply retiring with the various benefits that you've worked up over the years. Truckman, your boss, is a hell of a guy, and he takes care of those who come and go at Truckman Trucking. When you've put in the kind of time that you have, there's no doubt Truckman is going to have your back in the next phase of your life.

You knock twice on the door of your boss's office out of sheer courtesy, then barrel in before he has a chance to respond. Truckman is there waiting for you with a huge smile on his face, standing up from his desk and walking around to offer a warm hug. He's a large man with plenty of stubble, and you've never seen without a baseball hat on his head and a carton of chocolate milk in his hand.

Back in his day, Truckman was a trucker as well, hence the name, but now he's happy to stay here in the office headquarters and make sure the shipments come and go on time. He started on the ground floor and worked his way up to the top, something you've always deeply admired. It's part of the reason you trust him so much, and why you want to make sure you leave this job with a sparkling track record.

You've always made your delivery on time, come rain, sleet or snow, and that's exactly what you intend to do on this final mission.

"Whatdaya got for me?" you question. "What's the last ride gonna be?"

"A very important shipment," Truckman replies, releasing you from the hug and then strolling back over to his desk.

He grabs a clipboard covered in papers and hands it over to you, the manifest for what you'll be hauling on your final trek.

"Chocolate milk," you read aloud, smiling to yourself. Your first ever shipment was a truck full of chocolate milk, so it might as well be your last.

"From Billings to San Diego," Truckman replies, nodding. "This one is special, so I need someone I can trust."

There's something about this comment that strikes you as a bit odd. Part of the mission statement here at Truckman Trucking is that *every* shipment is important, so getting this reminder on your last day is a little unexpected.

"Of course," you reply. "It'll get it there."

"Seventy two hours," Truckman continues, the seriousness still haunting his expression and tone. "No less."

You nod in confirmation. "I won't let you down. This is my last shipment and I plan on going out with a perfect record."

"That's what I was counting on," your boss replies, his mood suddenly becoming jovial again as he slaps you on the back.

With that, you turn and head out of Truckman's office of the last time, strolling through the warehouse and eventually arriving at your rig. The vehicle has already been packed up and secured by your usual crew, but you still like do a personal round of checks before hitting the road. You make sure the tire pressure is where it needs to be, then open up the back to take a look at the payload for yourself.

There, stacked from floor to ceiling, are thousands upon thousands of glass chocolate milk bottles stacked in an icy cold refrigeration chamber. It's quite a sight, really, so many of the same thing crammed into one tiny space, and the sight of it brings you a strange sense of peace at the beginning of your journey. To a trucker like yourself, this is a blank canvas.

In addition to the chocolate milk, there's a trusty SPARE TRUCK TIRE, which you hopefully won't need to use.

You pull down the enormous rolling door of this cargo container and close it up, locking it tight and then heading back around to your familiar front cab.

With only three days to get to San Diego, the City of Beaches, you better get a move on.

There are two basic routes for this particular trip, which you've done plenty of times before.

Your first choice is to take the main highway through Idaho. This path is fairly direct and slightly faster than any other option. However, the fact that it's going to be your last ride weighs heavy on your decision. You'd like to see a bit of the glorious scenery around these parts, and the backroads of Wyoming are just the ticket in that case.

Heading through Wyoming won't be that much slower, and you'll still have plenty of time to get to your destination.

You put the truck in drive and make your choice.

Head through Idaho on page 106
Head through Wyoming on page 26

It takes a hearty amount of mental fortitude, but you somehow manage to pull yourself together and focus on the task at hand. Maybe it's the mission itself that keeps you in line, a singular goal to maintain at the forefront of your mind while everything else swirls past; a lighthouse in the storm.

You plow ahead as the sun disappears completely, but only a few miles have passed when disaster strikes.

Without warning, your headlights reveal a tire strip laid out across the road before you, a long thin row of spikes that are specifically designed to pierce the rubber of your tires.

There's a loud, earsplitting bang and now the truck is losing control, shuddering with terrifying power as you struggle to maintain a straight path along the empty highway. You can feel the back of your rig fishtailing from side to side, and for a moment you get a sense the whole thing is going to tip right over.

Fortunately, this doesn't happen.

Soon enough, you're pulling off onto the side of the road and slowing to a stop, the flap of a ragged tire sounding loud in your ear.

You open up the door to your cab and leap down onto the gravel to assess the damage. Your truck is built to withstand a lot, and the strip only managed to puncture one of your tires. Still, that's more than enough damage to keep you from going anywhere for the time being.

Even more pressing, however, is the terrifying question that repeats itself over and over again in your head, a warning alarm at the forefront of your mind. Who laid this trap?

Without warning, a pair of headlights slice through the darkness before you. The red and black Cobbler Trucking big-rig reveals its enormous and terrifying shape, parked on the side of the road just a few yards away. The vehicle begins to slowly creep forward.

Run off into the fields and hide on 169
Stay and confront them on page 188

You're not great at replacing a tire, but you're not terrible at it either. It's a risky move, and you can't believe you're actually considering it, but it's also the best option there is if you can pull it off.

When you finally decide it's safe to make your move, you sneak up very slowly and crack open the door of your truck cab. As quietly as possible, you lift down your spare truck tire and your tools, then immediately get to work.

The whole time, your heart is slamming within your chest, your senses on high alert as you go about your business. Every movement with your metal tools is breathtakingly careful, well aware that even the slightest knock of two object against one another could call out like a bell across the open plains.

Somehow, you eventually manage to put on the *SPARE TRUCK TIRE*, fixing your vehicle and allowing you the option of a safe escape.

Of course, the second you pull out and hit the road they can just chase you down again. You need to slow them down somehow, but at what cost?

As your eyes fall onto the other truck sitting empty before you, you hatch a plan. It's incredibly risky, but you *might* be able to sneak over there and steal their keys, rendering them unable to follow as you make a break for it.

Both options are potentially dangerous, but with time running down before the devil and the bigfoot return, you have to make a decision.

Just drive and get out of there on page 45
Take their keys so they can't follow you on page 102

The logical part of your brain knows that you should probably stay focused on the task at hand, but there's something about this bizarre, dancing illumination that takes hold of your curiosity and simply refuses to let go.

You climb out of your cab and lock up the truck, then begin your journey out into the tall grass. Your eyes quickly begin to adjust to the night, and while you still need to maintain a careful, slow pace, you do a pretty good job of getting where you're going. Fortunately, there's not much out here in the middle of nowhere for you to trip over or run into face first.

As you grow closer and closer to the light, you begin to hear the sweet sound of music floating across the plains. It's an upbeat song played on a fiddle, banjo and guitar, but there's also something distinctly haunting and melancholy about it.

Soon enough, you find yourself at the edge of a small ghost town, a collection of old wooden buildings set in the dirt around a central square, and not much else. The square is populated by several figures, however, and you gasp when you see them.

It appears there's a party going on, with singing and dancing abound. The revelers are all clad in old clothing, like settlers from way back when, and every single one of them sparkles with an eerie blue glow. Of course, it's not just the glow that gives them away as ghosts, it's also the fact they're all semi-transparent.

You freeze in your tracks, an icy bolt of fear shooting through your body as you realize what you've stumbled upon. It's fascinating to observe, but as someone who is not entirely familiar with the spirit world, you're not sure what will happen should they catch you.

This isn't a question that you have for long.

Suddenly, one of the ghostly dancers, a woman in a long white dress, turns and approaches you slowly. She's smiling wide, an expression that you can't seem to place as either sinister or inviting. One thing's for sure, though, the ghost is not at all alarmed to see you. It makes you wonder if she'd known you were hiding there the whole time.

"What are you doing here?" she demands to know, suddenly making her feelings very clear. "How dare you disturb the good people of Home of Truth?"

"I'm just..." you stammer, backing away as you shake your head from side to side. "I'm just passing through."

"A simple detour on your way to San Diego?" she hisses. "Is that all we are to you?"

"No!" you blurt.

Suddenly, the ghost's expression changes, softening into a face of good natured laughter. "I'm just messing with you," she offers. "I'm so sorry. There's not much to do when you're a ghost, so scaring people kinda becomes a habit."

"Oh," you reply in startled amazement, deeply thankful for this tonal shift. "Yeah, I bet. How'd you know I was headed to San Diego?"

"Ghosts have a strange relationship with timelines," she explains. "We're here now, but we can see into the past sometimes, or the future, or the potential."

"That's very confusing," you admit.

The ghostly woman nods. "I know. Some stuff will make sense before you ride the lonesome train, some stuff will make sense after, but you should rarely mix the two. For instance, I shouldn't tell you that you're actually just a character in a book."

"Wait, what?" you blurt.

"Oops. Nevermind," the phantom blurts, her eyes going wide.

She takes a moment to collect herself as the two of you stand in awkward silence.

"Anyway, you wanna dance?" the ghostly woman questions.

Decline on page 23
Accept her invitation on page 183

8

"Sure," you reply with a smile, not sure when you'll have another opportunity to share a dance with someone from beyond the grave.

You take the ghostly woman's hand in yours and soon enough the two of you have joined the other sprits, dancing and frolicking right there in the middle of Home of Truth's tiny town square. The other phantoms welcome you gladly, and it's not long before you've completely forgotten their otherworldly nature.

The band kicks into high gear, segueing into one song after another as you twist and twirl the night away. They clap their hands and stomp their feet jovially shouting out words of encouragement to their new friend.

Even after the dancing has finished, you stick around a while to chat with the citizens of this ghostly hamlet, trading stories as you offer up tales of your days on the road.

It's a wonderful time, but as the night wears on you eventually realize that you've gotta pull yourself away.

When you tell the ghosts that it's your time to go they all boo loudly, then accept this reality and offer you a series of kind goodbyes.

The last to see you off is the ghostly woman who you first danced with, a spirit you now know as Remla.

"Have a good trip," the phantom offers warmly. "I know I told you the timelines of the dead and the living shouldn't cross, but you're just so kind. I'd like to offer up a little more advice."

"Are you sure that's alright?" you question.

Remla shrugs. "Who knows? What I *do* know is that if you ever find yourself in a casino, don't go with the unicorns if you can help it. Don't run through the garden either, head toward the pool."

"That... makes no sense," you reply, "but maybe in the future?"

"There are some potential timelines where it might come in handy," the friendly ghost offers with a grin, then raises a finger to her lips as though to remind you of this information's secret nature. "Goodbye," she eventually offers, then drifts back to her spectral party.

You turn and begin the trek back to your truck, thankful for this unique and fulfilling experience. It's a long walk through the field of grass, and it gives you a moment to refocus your mind. It's time to concentrate on making this delivery.

Suddenly, you stop, gazing out at the road that rests several yards ahead of you. Your truck is right where you left it, but another vehicle sits parked nearby with its headlights blaring. It's the truck from Cobbler Trucking.

You duck down into the tall grass as two figures slowly walk out into their own headlights, talking amongst themselves as the they formulate a plan.

You can't make out their words from all the way over here, but you *do* manage to get a good look at the frightening characters. The first is a tall and rather imposing bigfoot, clad in a dark leather jacket and sporting an enormous beard that hangs down the front of his hairy, muscular body. He has an eye patch over one eye, which gives him a distinctly piratelike appearance.

The second backlit figure to emerge from the darkness is a bright red devil, a humanoid figure with stark black hair and two long, curved horns. He has a slender tail with a point at the end, which lashes around his legs as he walks. The devil is wearing a short sleeved button up shirt, and over the heart is a name tag patch that you can just barely make out. It simply reads 'Ted.'

After a bit of discussion the bigfoot strolls around to the back of your truck. He picks up a large rock from the side of the road and smashed open the lock, then rolls up the door to your cargo container with a loud rattle.

Next the bigfoot climbs up into the back of the truck and begins to go through your shipment, tearing open the crates of delicious chocolate milk and tossing them out onto the road behind with a series of horrific smashes and crunches. You watch with absolute disgust as the entire contents of your truck is emptied out before you, all of that glorious chocolate milk gone to waste as it pours across the glass covered ground below.

As the anger within you builds, you seriously consider marching over there and giving them a piece of your mind, but you muster up all the discipline you can manage and hold yourself back. Something much more important is at play.

"The device isn't here," the one-eyed bigfoot eventually calls out.

"What?" Ted erupts angrily. "This is the truck! It has to be there!"

The devil who had been waiting around this time now springs into action, making his way around to the back of the truck and having a look for himself. The two of them continue to search, growing more and more frustrated by the second.

As someone spying on them from afar, this frustration only helps your cause. Their tone is much louder now, heightened to a point that you can easily hear them.

"There must be a secret door!" Ted cries out. "There's magic afoot."

"You know magic, though," the bigfoot retorts. "You can dispel it!"

"Not this powerful!" Ted continues, his voice bubbling over with absolute rage. "Find the driver! They must know the way in!"

The two figures hop down out of the back of your truck. "You go that way and I'll go this way," you hear the bright red devil instruct, the two of them splitting off in either direction to search the field.

Fortunately, neither one of them is wandering off in your exact direction yet, and there's plenty of ground for them to cover. If you stay here long enough, they're certain to find you, but at least you've got a moment to think.

At this point, a few courses of action come to mind.

The simplest answer is to make a run for it out here in the field, leaving your rig behind and waiting until the coast is clear to make your return. Maybe you could even sprint back to the ghost's and ask for their help.

Of course, the longer these two unsavory characters have your truck in their possession, the more likely they are to find the secret compartment.

One solution might be to creep over there and find the device this devil and his bigfoot companion are looking for before they ever get a chance to steal it themselves.

The bravest answer, however, is the most tempting and the most dangerous. As the bigfoot and the devil get farther and farther away from their own vehicle, it crosses your mind that you could sneak over there, snatch their keys, then take off in your own truck while leaving them stranded.

The only thing for certain is that you can't wait any longer to act.

Run away through the field on page 32
Search for the secret compartment yourself on page 180
Steal their keys and hit the road on page 48

"Okay, let's do it," you reply, finally accepting the offer.

"Yes!" the living corn cries out excitedly. "This is going to be great!"

"Thank you," you continue, still not feeling quite right about accepting the generosity of your new friend. Her kindness is appreciated, and you want to make sure she knows that.

Soon enough, you and the sentient corn are driving down the Las Vegas strip, cruising toward your destination at The Grand Buckaroo Hotel And Casino. Once there, the two of you will immediately head to the World Series Of Blackjack sign-in table and get started, but until then you sit back and enjoy the brilliant flashing lights of this truly unique city.

Your gaze jumps from one side of the street to the other as you take it all in, appreciating the glitz and the glamor of this desert town built on hard luck and good fun.

It's not long before you see the brilliant glittering neon of The Grand Buckaroo, this behemoth hotel towering above you with its notorious waving cowboy all lit up in yellow and orange. Michelle pulls into the parking structure, which winds in and out of the building and eventually leads you deep down into the depths of the casino.

Michelle eventually pulls into her parking spot and the two of you climb out, hearts pounding with excitement as you make your way toward the casino floor. While it had taken Michelle a while to convince you, you're now fully on board with this adventure, trying your best to remained focused on the competition ahead.

While this might seem like a deviation from the important journey at hand, it's really not. If you can win the grand prize then your transportation to San Diego is automatically taken care of.

Eventually, you and the sentient corn find the sign-in counter and approach it confidently. You fill out a small bit of paperwork, then Michelle hands over your buy-in cash.

"Here you go," the woman at the desk offers, printing out two tickets and presenting one to each of you. These slips feature a randomly generated seat assignment at one of the various blackjack tables, and you quickly discover that you and your new friend are quite far away from each other.

"Good luck," you offer, giving Michelle a warm hug.

"Break a leg," she replies with a smile.

The two of you part ways and soon enough you find yourself wandering over to an empty seat. You double check this is the correct spot, still feeling incredibly nervous but trying your best to stay cool, then sit down like you know what you're doing.

You give the other four players at this small table a nod.

"I'm Keith," says the player right next to you, a sentient jet plane with a handsome face and a wide smile. He extends a wing and you shake it firmly. "Nice to meet you."

"You too," you offer in return. "How's it going so far?"

Keith shrugs. "Competition just stared, but I'm feeling good."

The sentient vehicle nods at the stack of chips in front of him, which is significantly more than the rest of the players.

"Whoa," you blurt. "How'd you manage that?"

"Well, I'm a pretty good card counter," Keith admits.

Your eyes go wide as you glance over at the dealer, shocked the jet plane would just reveal this out loud. The dealer doesn't react.

"It's not illegal," Keith continues, "Just discouraged. For these competitions, however, The Grand Buckaroo Casino says that card counting is fair game."

"Oh, whoa," you reply. "I didn't know that."

"That's not even my real secret weapon," Keith admits.

You lean in a little closer, hoping this friendly sentient plane will offer you a bit of his wisdom. "What is?" you question.

"I just play with love," Keith continues. "If I get in a bad mood then I know it's time to leave. As long as I'm playing with love, I tend to do pretty well."

"I'll give it a try," you reply.

"Good," Keith offers with a smile, then nods at the felted green table. "Because you're up."

"Oh!" you blurt, glancing back at the two cards sitting before you.

The dealer stares at you with a devastatingly expressionless face. "Would you like to hit or stand?" they ask.

Your blackjack knowledge suddenly flashes before your eyes, a split second refresher on how to play that's there and gone before you even have a chance to acknowledge it.

"Uh... hit," you reply.

The dealer lays down another card, bringing your total to twenty one. That's a good thing.

"Nice work," the jet plane leans over to whisper in your year. "You're gonna do just fine."

You continue playing throughout the evening, trusting your instincts and trying your best to remember Keith's advice about playing with love in your heart. Eventually, the other players begin to lose all of their chips and slip away, while the stacks belonging to you and your new jet plane friend seem to only grow steadily larger.

Soon enough, the dealers take a break and your chips are collected and moved over to a final table.

You have five minutes to grab a snack or stretch your legs, and during this time Michelle the sentient corn approaches you with some bad news.

"I just lost," she offers.

"I'm so sorry!" you blurt.

Michelle shrugs, clearly just in it for the fun and not really caring that she's missed out on any prizes. "I was playing well, I just got unlucky," she offers. "That's the key to these final tables, you've gotta have a little luck on your side."

Suddenly, a bell rings, alerting you that the competition will begin again in thirty seconds.

"You better get back there," the living corn reminds you.

You smile and part ways, but her comments about luck still hang in the back of your mind.

If you have no lucky items, turn to page 153
If you have the lucky jackalope's foot turn to page 28
If you have the lucky unicorn shoe turn to page 158

After the drama earlier in your day, it's nice to settle in and just drive for a while. You feel comfortable here behind the wheel, and as the sun creeps its way across the sky you get a chance to finally meditate on the fact that this is really your final ride.

It's been a long road to travel, both literally and otherwise, but you're happy to look back on your journey and say that you did things right. You always made the delivery.

The gorgeous landscape gradually begins to shift and change as you cross the state line into Utah. Here, you find yourself greeted by wide open fields of seed grass that stretch on and on as far as the eye can see. In every direction, the beautiful plains seem to wave happily as you pass them by, seeing you off.

As the sun dips just below the horizon line and the sky blooms a deep purple, you find yourself bathed in a sensation of peace and tranquility.

Suddenly, however, that all changes. You glance in your rearview mirror to catch another set of headlights approaching, and approaching fast. You're not going slow by any means, which implies this visitor is coming up behind you at well over the speed limit.

Soon enough, they're pulling up in the lane right next to you. In the dying light of the day you get a full view of the enormous, black and red semi-truck, this vehicle emblazoned on the side with a familiar logo.

"Cobbler Trucking," you read aloud under your breath, immediately recognizing a member of your main competitor's fleet.

If it was up to you, you'd welcome another trucking line, and often times this is the case. There's a trucker code out here on the road, and you're always willing to help out a fellow driver in need, even if they're driving for someone else.

However, Cobbler Trucking is a different kind of monster. Everyone knows them for their bad attitude and occasional dastardly deed, a crew of hateful pirates on the highways of America.

Suddenly, the truck blasts its horn. The sound is so loud and abrupt that you jump in your seat and jerk the wheel, your heart skipping a beat as you struggle to collect yourself and keep from running off the road.

Seconds later, the rival truck takes off ahead of you, slamming on the gas and erupting onward at a reckless speed. You watch as they disappear into the distance ahead, eventually vanishing into the night.

16

You take a deep breath and let it out, still feeling incredibly on edge. Earlier in the drive you did a good job of blocking out the trauma of that disappearing potato, but in this moment of weakness your anxiety all comes flooding back.

"Oh shit, oh shit," you start repeating under your breath, unable to stop the words from spilling out of your mouth.

You've still got plenty of ground to cover if you want to make this delivery, but part of you is begging for a break. Maybe the safest option is to pull over and gather your thoughts for a minute.

You notice a small turnout up ahead, a perfect spot to take a breather should you need it.

The turnout is on page 81
Push through and keep driving on page 120

You decide to heed the dinosaur's warning, pulling the front end of your truck slowly into the stegosaurus's rather large auto garage, which is directly attached to the gas station shop.

You park your vehicle and climb out, thanking the dinosaur as he gets to work.

There's a bench nearby, only partially covered by tools and oil cans, and you take a seat right here. You watch as the mechanic goes about his business, first investigating the back of the truck and then making his way around to the hood. The dinosaur pops it open and climbs up onto the front bumper, staring down into the belly of your vehicle.

"Oh yeah," the stegosaurus suddenly blurts, clearly noticing that something is amiss. "Just like I thought."

"What is it?" you question.

The prehistoric creature turns back toward you. "Somebody must want a piece of your cargo," he explains. "They cut the brake line. Probably hoping to run you off the road a little way down the hill and then steal from the wreckage."

"Oh my god," you exclaim, your eyes going wide.

"Come on up here and take a look," the stegosaurus continues, motioning for you to join him.

You do as instructed, climbing up onto your bumper next to the dinosaur and peering down withing the inner workings of your truck. Sure enough, you can see the brake lines have been severed.

"From the looks of it this was not a clean cut," the stegosaurus explains. "Looks like something pointy was rubbed back and forth across them until they snapped."

"Rubbed back and forth?" you repeat, deeply confused by the implication of this.

"Antlers," the dinosaur explains. "Looks like a pack of jackalopes to me."

While you've never seen a jackalope before in real life, you're heard plenty of stories about these giant rabbits with sharp, pointy antlers sprouting from the top of their heads.

While some claim this society of wild creatures is mischievous and fun, other's describe their actions as downright criminal. It looks as though the latter were right.

"So they're real," you exclaim. "I wasn't sure if Jackalopes were actual creatures, or just an old legend."

"Oh, they're real," the dinosaur replies, then nods over your shoulder at the wall behind you.

You follow the dinosaur's gaze and yelp in shock when you spot the mounted head of a jackalope, antlers and all.

The stegosaurus laughs. "You think that's something, wait 'til you see my collection of lucky jackalope's feet. We sell them in the shop. Go in there and fetch yourself one, it's on me."

You climb down from your place on the front of the truck, still a little in shock from what you've just seen, then wander through a door that separates the auto garage from the gas station connivence shop.

You find a LUCKY JACKALOPE'S FOOT hanging among some assorted charms and take it for yourself.

Just then, a bell jingles as someone enters the shop.

"Tell them I'll be out in a minute," the dinosaur calls over to you from the garage, his head still buried within the hood of your big-rig.

A figure approaches you now, strangely tall and wrapped up in a long black trench coat. They're wearing a hat with a wide brim, the tip of it pulled down to cover up their face and obscure them in shadow.

"He said he'll be out in a moment," you offer this unknown visitor. "He's just back in the garage finishing up some work."

"Maybe you can help me," the figure in the trench coat begins, their voice coming out as a strange, sing-song gargle. "My car broke down right outside. Do you know anything about cars?"

"A little," you admit, "but I'm not the expert here."

"Oh that's fine," the lanky figure offers in return, waving away your concerns. "I just need a second set of eyes."

Go out there and take a look on page 121
Suggest waiting for the actual mechanic on page 109

Despite the trust in your loaders back at the warehouse, you're well aware that accidents happen and things could've shifted during this first leg of the drive. It could also be absolutely nothing, but the few minutes it takes for your new potato friend to climb back there and check things out isn't going to make a dent in your drivetime.

"Alright, sure," you finally reply, nodding at the living vegetable.

The two of you head out and make your away around to the back of the big-rig. The enormous cargo container that makes up the latter half of this vehicle features an enormous rolling gate, which you quickly unlock and then fling upward with a loud, rumbling crash.

Packed tightly into the back of truck are more chocolate milk bottles than you can fathom. They sit there in the icy cool air of the refrigerated chamber, looking absolutely spectacular as they patiently wait for their final destination.

The sentient potato climbs up onto the lip of the truck next to you, her hundreds of eyes working over your cargo with a deep observational intensity. She's seeing so much more than you could ever imagine, taking it in and cataloging even the smallest details.

"I need to go deeper," the vegetable informs you.

Before you have a chance to respond, she's jumping up and grabbing ahold of a chocolate milk stack, hoisting her large rounded body up over the edge and then sliding across the top.

"Wait!" you blurt out, then realize your protests are useless now that the sentient veggie has disappeared over the side of the crates. The glass bottles rattle loudly within their containers, causing you to wince and tense up, but not a single one of them cracks.

The potato pops her head out over the edge of a crate suddenly. "What was that?" she questions.

"Oh... nothing," you finally reply, just going with it.

The vegetable nods and then heads back in, climbing across the top. You can hear her rattling along, then suddenly stopping once she reaches the center of the truck.

"Oh whoa," is all you can make out, her voice muffled and distant. For a moment it sounds as though she's climbed down off the crates, but that shouldn't be possible. There's no empty space back there.

"What is it?" you call.

"I think there's a secret compartment in your truck!" the living potato yells back. "Most people wouldn't notice it, but these eyes can see everything. There's a magic security lock."

"A magic what?" you blurt.

"Probably needs three knocks and a password," the potato continues. "Unless I can figure out the lock mechanism just by looking at it."

Soon enough, the vegetable's voice lowers a bit as she begins talking to herself, going over some difficult mental problem-solving equation in her head.

"Are you okay?" you continue, still trying to figure out what's going on.

"Yeah!" the voice offers. "I think I've figured it out!"

"Figured what out?" you question.

Suddenly, a loud, sizzling zap erupts from somewhere in the middle of the cargo hold. From where you stand you can see a brilliant blue light erupt from between the bottles, nearly causing you to stumble backward off the edge of the vehicle as you shield your eyes.

You manage to stay upright, however, hanging onto a conveniently placed handle on the side of the truck.

The next think you know, you're plunged into silence.

"Are you okay?" you call out.

No response.

"Hello?" you continue.

Still no response.

Eventually, you take matters into your own hands, climbing up over the top of the chocolate milk crates and then shimmying along like your living potato friend had done just moments earlier.

When you reach the middle of the truck you gasp aloud, discovering there is, in fact, a giant empty space where no cargo has been placed. The potato was right.

Even more bizarre, however, is that fact that your new vegetable friend has disappeared completely.

"Where did you go?" you cry, still finding nothing but silence in return.

You search around for the potato a bit longer, then eventually realize she's truly gone. Maybe this was just some kind of prank, which is seeming more and more likely now that you've had a chance to look around and determine there's no secret passage back here.

At least, no secret passage that you can find.

After moving some of the chocolate milk crates into a better position and evening out your load, you finally climb out from the back of your truck. You wipe the grease and dirt off your hands and then call out one last time for the potato.

"If you're in there, let me know!" you yell. "I need to close up!"

This time you wait extra long, but still no response comes. Eventually, you shut the back of the truck and lock it, then make your way up to the front cab once again.

You pull out your phone and dial Truckman.

"Hello?" comes a familiar voice at the end of the line.

"What's going on with my truck?" you demand to know.

Truckman hesitates a moment, taking his time before responding. "You found out, huh?"

"Well, I found out the pack job was messed up," you explain. "I also made a potato disappear."

"A what?" Truckman replies, confused.

"A potato," you repeat, then suddenly clarify. "A living potato."

"Oh no," Truckman blurts. "Did they get into the secret compartment?"

"So there is a secret compartment!" you question.

Truckman's tone shifts a bit, realizing now that the circumstances of his original assignment for you have changed.

"Listen, you're not just shipping chocolate milk," Truckman finally admits. "You're carrying something very, very important back there, something that could alter the fate of this entire reality. Hell, it could alter *every* reality!"

"What is it?" you question, frustrated, "and why didn't you tell me?"

"I didn't wanna tell you because that puts you in danger," Truckman continues. "The less you know, the better. If you we're to get captured, that's not information you want lurking in the back of your mind. As long as you don't know, then dark wizards can't extract the information."

"Dark wizards are after me?" you cry out in alarm.

"I don't know," Truckman continues. "Just... trust me on this. It's very, very important that you get this delivery to San Diego. The fate of the universe depends on it."

You take a deep breath and let it out, remembering all the times Truckman has had your back in the past. "Okay," you finally reply.

"If that potato was pure of heart then they're fine," Truckman explains. "You just need to keep that cargo from falling into the wrong hands."

You feel the trucker's code tugging at your heartstrings and pushing you onward. You didn't ask to be thrust into this situation, but you've made a commitment to the journey. Once a truck leaves the warehouse under your command, you'll get it to its destination even if it's the last thing you do.

This is your final ride, anyway. You might as well make it count.

"You can count on me," you state firmly.

"Thanks," Truckman offers. "Keep in touch."

You hang up the phone and then put your vehicle into drive. You pull away from the travel stop, headed for Utah.

Continue to Utah on page 15

The offer to stick around is nice enough, but you can't help shake the feeling that this little detour has already consumed too much of your time. You've got an important mission to take care of, and as exciting as this all is, you really should get going.

Besides, dancing with a ghost seems like an activity that could have unintended consequences on the living. That's not exactly a theory you feel like testing right now.

"Thanks, but I really should be going," you insist, stepping back from the phantom woman.

She's a little disappointed, but manages a smile and a shrug. "I knew you we're gonna say that," she replies, then floats back to the rest of her group as they greet her warmly and fall into another rousing dance routine.

You turn and begin the trek back to your truck, retracing your steps through this wide open field of darkness. You walk for quite a while until, suddenly, you notice something on the road ahead.

Your truck is right where you left it, but another vehicle sits parked nearby with its headlights blaring. It's the truck from Cobbler Trucking.

"Oh shit," you blurt, seconds from ducking down into the tall grass before two large, hairy hands suddenly grab you from behind.

Your immediate instinct is squirm away, kicking and screaming as you fight off this mysterious attacker, but it quickly becomes apparent that he's just too strong for you to contend with. The enormous figure begins to carry you back across the field, his huge furry arms making it immediately apparent that this unexpected guest is a bigfoot.

From what you can make out, he seems to be wearing a leather jacket and sporting a patch over one eye.

Eventually, you reach the road, where the bigfoot finally sets you down in front of another mysterious stranger.

"Caught them in the field," the bigfoot states gruffly.

You look up to see a bright red devil standing before you, a humanoid figure with stark black hair and two long, curved horns. He has a slender, forked tail with a point at the end, which lashes around his legs as he walks. The devil is wearing a short sleeved button up shirt, and over the heart is a name tag patch that you can just barely make out. It simply reads 'Ted.'

"Where's the device," the devil demands to know.

"What device?" you question.

"The button," Ted continues sternly.

You shake your head profusely. "I don't know, I'm just driving a shipment of chocolate milk. I have no idea what you're talking about."

The devil grins. "Then why is the truck empty?"

"The milk was stolen," you explain desperately. "It should be full!"

"But you're still headed toward San Diego?" Ted continues. "Something doesn't add up here, but it will soon enough."

The bigfoot behind you steps forward a bit, trying his best to be imposing and doing a damn good job. "Should I smash them to bits?" the bigfoot questions.

Ted shakes his head. "Not yet. We might need some help getting this thing open."

Suddenly, Ted thrusts his hands out toward you as a cascade of swirling green energy erupts from his fingertips, wrapping itself around your body and pulling tight. You cry out in surprise as your form begins to change shape, shrinking down and pulling inward as your skin hardens into scale. The sound of your voice begins to morph until it shifts into a long hiss, and soon enough you find yourself lying flat in the middle of the road, staring up from a new, much smaller body.

Ted has turned you into a snake.

While these reptiles are quite fast if they want to be, you're too shocked to take any immediate action. Before you get a chance to slither away, the giant, one-eyed bigfoot reaches down and grabs ahold of your long green body, picking you up and dropping you into a bucket.

You open your mouth to cry out, but can't find a way to form the words. Instead, you focus this energy into climbing out and escaping, but the bigfoot swiftly covers the top of your container with a sturdy piece of flat wood.

There's a series of loud clangs and eventually the cacophony of your truck roaring to life, hotwired up and ready to go. It appears both vehicles are prepped and ready for the journey ahead.

Moments later, the weight of your bucket begins to shift. You're being lifted in the air and carried somewhere, then set down roughly on what you can only assume is a truck bench.

The familiar rumble of a motor beneath your body lets you know that you're on your way.

Continue onward in your bucket to page 157

It's your last drive, so you decide to make it an enjoyable one. You have no intention of this being your first late delivery, but the scenic route is worth a few extra hours so long as everything gets where it needs to be.

Soon enough, you find yourself cruising through the glorious mountain passes of Wyoming, The Why State, gazing out at the snow covered landscape of lush green trees and enormous cracked boulders.

You're peacefully lost in your thoughts, but eventually something begins to pull you back into the present. You can't help but notice that another truck appears to be following you. It's quite a ways back, but it always seems to be there in the mirror just rumbling along.

Of course, this is a very common trucking route, and it's not unheard of for you to notice other vehicles tagging along for an entire cross country journey. However, something about this just feels different. It's hard to make out the vehicle's colors from this far away, but they appear to be a combination of blood red and jet black.

You continue to glance in the rear view mirror as you speed up a bit, pushing the gas and eventually pulling away from this mysterious truck. Soon enough, it's nothing but a distant memory.

Of course, speeding up like this has more advantages than just losing a possible tail: it also gets you where you're going that much quicker. When you finally pull off the road for a tank of gas, you're pleasantly surprised by just how deep into the Wyoming wilderness you've managed to travel.

You climb out of your cab and stroll over to the pump, getting down to business as you fill your tank. You feel relaxed and care free, whistling to yourself as you watch a small handful of delicate snowflakes drifting down from above.

Eventually, your gaze comes to rest on the stegosaurus who runs this gas station. He's staring past you, then suddenly locks eyes.

"Hey! Someone's messing with your truck!" the prehistoric creature calls out.

You immediately turn around, glancing over in the direction this stegosaurus was so keen on observing.

"Back there?" you question, pointing down the length of your enormous vehicle.

The dinosaur nods. "Yep."

"I don't see anything," you call out in return, your tank finally filling to the brim. You pull out the nozzle and hang it up, anxious to continue on your way.

The gas station attendant notices you heading for your cab once more. "Wait!" he cries. "You really shouldn't keep going in this weather if someone messed with your truck. I saw them in the back, but they could've gotten anywhere."

You stop, still not entirely convinced this dinosaur isn't just messing with you. "What should I do then?" you call back to him.

The stegosaurus motions toward a garage just a few feet away, the building connected to his gas station convenience store. "We do mechanic work here. Pull your rig in and I'll take a look. I'll give you a deal."

Keep trucking on page 85
Head into the auto shop on page 17

Remembering that you've got a lucky jackalope's foot in your pocket, you pull it out and give the furry nub a massage with your fingers, hoping to brush off a little of the magic for yourself.

Who knows if it actually works.

You sit back down at the blackjack table just in time for the game to start up yet again, the cards coming out and everyone taking a look at what they've got. There's a slight gasp when your two cards are revealed.

"Blackjack," the dealer announces, handing over your full bet plus a little extra for your big win.

Surely this must be a coincidence, you think, but after the next few hands you begin to suspect that your lucky jackalope's foot might be working a lot harder than you initially thought.

Gradually, the other players start to bust out, dropping the field down to just you and Keith the jet plane.

"I've gotta say, and I mean this in the nicest way possible, you're the luckiest person I've ever met," Keith informs you. "You've been on a hell of a run."

"Thanks," you reply, not knowing what else to say.

The dealer suddenly interrupts your conversation, motioning toward Keith. "Would you like to hit or stand?" he questions.

"I don't care," Keith replies with a shrug.

"You need to choose, sir," the dealer continues.

The jet plane laughs, amused. "I quit then, give my friend here the grand prize."

Your eyes go wide. "Wait, what?" you blurt.

"It's fine," Keith explains "I'm a billionaire already. I just do The World Series Of Blackjack for fun."

Alarm bells start going off as confetti begins to fall from the ceiling above you.

"We have a winner!" the dealer announces, springing to his feet.

You stand up as a crowd of onlookers begin to clap excitedly. You'd certainly hoped to make it this far, but now that you're here at the top it seems like some kind of bizarre dream.

You reach into your pocket and give the luck jackalope's foot one last rub of thanks.

Suddenly, the commotion of bells and whistles around you is cut by the roar of a powerful engine. You glance over to see a beautiful chrome sportscar rolling down an isle of slot machines, its gull-wing doors opening up and beckoning you within.

"Hey there," comes a soft, silky voice from the vehicle. "I'm Riley, the car."

"Oh, hi!" you blurt in response.

"Wanna get out of here?" she continues.

You turn around and thank Keith the billionaire jet plane for kindly dropping out, saying your goodbyes and then climbing into the driver's seat of this incredible, futuristic vehicle. An assortment of screens and readouts appear before you, popping up like the holographic displays in some science fiction masterpiece.

"Just so you know, there's a unit of unicorn security guards approaching from the east," Riley informs you. "They're coming to haul you in for cheating."

"Wait, what?" You blurt, utterly confused.

A display suddenly pops up of six unicorns in a dark suits and sunglasses pushing their way through the crowd of gamblers. "Judging by their elevated heart rates and the dilation of their pupils, I can tell they're preparing to lie to you," the sentient car continues. "You have not actually been caught cheating. It's a ruse."

"But why?" you question aloud.

"I'm not sure, maybe they're working for someone who has it out for you?" Riley offers. "I don't think we should stick around and find out."

A chill runs down your spine as you hear this, realizing now that Ted could be lurking somewhere nearby. "You're right, let's get out of here."

You throw the car into drive and take off through the casino, rumbling out into the hotel lobby and then just barely fitting through a set of wide doors to the outside world.

You glance in the rearview mirror to see the unicorns sprinting after you, but now that you're out on the Las Vegas Strip you have plenty of room to pick up speed. With a loud roar from Riley's engine the two of you erupt forward, the force of your momentum pulling you back against the seat behind you.

You'll be in San Diego in no time.

30

It's sunrise as you pull up to the wharf, the glorious ocean stretching out before you as golden sunlight dances across the waves. Your windows down, you can already sense to wonderful feeling of sea air against your face, and only wish the circumstances were less tense for you to enjoy it.

Before you is a large industrial warehouse constructed from cheap metal sheets and typically used to hold boats or maybe even huge commerical crates as they wait for a shipment transfer. This is the address.

You glance down at your phone, reminding yourself of the scientist that you're looking for. Truckman has sent you a photograph, and you read the name below it aloud.

"Borson Reems," you say, taking in this middle-aged man's enormous white beard and round nose. He has a kindness in his expression that is truly something to behold.

Riley emits a strange, dancing collection of laser beams from her dashboard, the array sweeping across the face of your phone as she scans the image.

"There are two lifeforms within the building who match this photograph," Riley announces.

"Two?" you blurt. "What do you mean?"

Another holographic display suddenly appears before you, floating in the air as a three dimensional projection of the warehouse. You can clearly see a man who looks like Borson Rooms standing in the middle of the room, but a projection of this same figure is also tied to a chair and gagged in a nearby closet. Also lurking in the shadows is the sturdy frame of a large, hairy bigfoot.

"It's a trap," you realize.

"I also detect a rather large big-rig parked on the other side of this structure," Riley announces. "I could hack into its navigation system and provide a great distraction, but only if the truck is turned on. We'd need the keys."

If you have the devil keys turn to page 91
If you don't have the devil keys turn to page 51

It's hard to believe how much your life has changed over the last year, but you're equally astonished at how much things have stayed the same.

During your last ride as a trucker you were constantly thinking about how much you'd miss the travel, the new locations and exciting adventures that would spring up at a moment's notice. Fortunately, this is something your new life as a card counter has in spades, and without the restrictions of sitting behind the wheel of an enormous vehicle all day to get there.

You think all this as you gaze down at the world below, sipping on your cold chocolate milk and enjoying the view from within your friend and coworker, Keith the jet plane. The two of you are headed off to Atlantic City for the weekend, and you couldn't be happier.

"How's it going back their?" Keith questions.

"Great," you reply. "Just thinking about the old days."

"Back when you saved all of existence?" Keith continues.

You laugh. It sounds ridiculous when it's put so bluntly, but you suppose he's right.

"Me and you play some high stakes cards," you reply, "but I guess the stakes aren't *that* high."

You take a deep breath and let it out, sinking into your chair a little deeper. You've adventured enough, you realize. Maybe now it's finally time to relax a bit.

THE END

You take off running, bolting through the field as fast as you can in the exact opposite direction. Even though your movements are not at all subtle, the darkness and the tall grass should cover your tracks and hopefully give you enough time to put some distance between you and your pursuers.

Of course, you'd hoped they might not notice you at all, but it quickly becomes apparent this is not the case.

"Over there!" the bigfoot shouts gruffly.

You suddenly get a sense that someone is sprinting behind you now, cutting through the field at an incredible speed as their feet slam hard against the soft dirt ground. They're gaining on you like an unescapable force of nature, a powerful hunter that simply cannot be beaten no matter how hard you try.

You're pushing with everything you've got, but a panic sets in as you realize that it might not be enough.

Suddenly, you trip, not because something grabs you but because your leg isn't quite where you expect it to be. You glance down in confusion to see that a sparkling green mist is swirling around you, spilling across your body in magical waves and somehow distorting your form. You're shrinking and contorting, and as you cry out in fear your voice begins to change as well. Your vocalization shifts from a human call to the hiss of a snake.

Ted strolls up and smiles in the moonlight, looming over you now that you've shrunken to a small fraction of your size. He reaches down and wraps his clawed devil hand around you, lifting you up, and as you struggle to get away you realize that your arms and legs have disappeared completely.

He's transformed you into a snake.

"Oh no you don't," Ted offers, chuckling to himself. "We don't want you slithering away in the grass. We might need you to open up that secret compartment for us, it depends on what Bazara the lock wizard says."

The devil holds you up, looking you in the eye as your forked tongue begins to flick the air involuntarily.

Moments later, the bigfoot with a patch over one eye steps up behind Ted, holding a bucket and a piece of wood in his hands. Ted drops you into the bucket and his bigfoot assistant places wood over the top like a lid.

Soon enough, you're listening to the sound of tall grass rushing across the plastic surface that surrounds you.

Eventually, the grass gives way. You're back at the road.

"You take that one," Ted commands.

There's a series of loud clangs and eventually you're treated to the sound of your truck roaring to life, hotwired up and ready to go. It appears both vehicles are prepped and ready for the journey ahead.

Moments later, the weight of your bucket begins to shift. You're being lifted in the air and carried somewhere, then set down roughly on what you can only assume is a truck bench.

The familiar rumble of a motor beneath your body lets you know that you're on your way.

Continue onward in your bucket to page 157

There's no way you can take on all six of these creatures by yourself, and as much as you'd like to fight them off and end this quickly, that just doesn't seem like a good plan.

"Okay," you finally reply.

Your hands in the air, you trudge around to the back of your truck as the creatures follow closely behind with their sharpened antlers at the ready. When you arrive at the large, roll-up door, you reach into your pocket and pull out the keys, then undo the lock. Reluctantly, you grip the bottom of the door and throw it upward with a loud clatter, revealing a stash of glorious brown chocolate milk crates stacked high within the refrigerated interior.

Instantly, the jackalopes begin to push past you, springing up into the cargo hold and getting to work. They create a long chain of unloaders, pulling the first crate down and then passing it off to the next creature in line. When a crate of milk reaches the final jackalope they will hop away over the snow drift, carrying it off into the frozen landscape.

You step back a bit, getting out of their way as the creatures continue about their business. It's not long before the entire truck is completely empty.

The jackalope leader hops over to you as the rest of the antlered beasts disappear into the wilds from which they came.

"Sorry about that," he offers in his gurgling, sing-song tone.

You say nothing in return as the jackalope hops off, leaving you standing here in the cold with a completely empty truck, your chocolate milk shipment long gone.

Not knowing what else to do, you return to your tools and keep repairing the vehicle. The longer you stay out here in the snow, the colder things are gonna get.

Eventually, you manage to return your brake lines to their former glory, then check around for any other problems. Once determining that everything is ship shape and ready for the road, you climb back into the cab of your truck and start things up.

While lesser vehicles might be trapped in this situation, your truck is built for power. It takes a minute, but eventually you manage to back yourself up out of the ditch and return to the asphalt. Soon enough, you're off and running.

Now for the hardest part. You call Truckman.

"Hey! What's going on?" your boss offers from the other end of the line, picking up swiftly.

"The truck is empty," you reply.

"What?" Truckman blurts, his vocalization one of utter horror. "Please tell me you're joking."

"Not joking," you continue. "A bunch of jackalopes cut my brakes and ran me off the road. They stole everything."

Truckman takes a long, deep breath, collecting his thoughts. "You okay?" he finally questions.

You realize that you're not even sure about this one, checking in with your body and mind for a moment.

"Yeah, I'm fine," you eventually reply.

"Listen to me very closely," Truckman continues. "When they were back there, did they find any secret magical compartments?"

"Uh... I don't think so," you reply, surprised by the direction these questions have gone.

"We're you watching them unload?" Truckman asks. "Did you see anything strange?"

"I was watching them," you reply confidently. "Nothing strange happened. Other than begin robbed by a pack of jackalopes."

Truckman breathes a huge sigh of relief. "You're not just shipping chocolate milk," your boss finally admits. "You're shipping something very, very important back there, something that could alter the fate of this entire reality. Hell, it could alter every reality!"

"What is it?" you question, utterly shocked, "and why didn't you tell me?"

"I didn't wanna tell you because that puts you in danger," Truckman continues. "The less you know, the better. If you we're to get captured, that's not information you want lurking in the back of your mind. If you don't know, then dark wizards can't extract the information."

"Dark wizards are after me?" you cry out in alarm.

"I don't know," Truckman continues. "Just... trust me on this one. It's very, very important for you to get that delivery to San Diego. The fate of the universe depends on it."

You take a deep breath and let it out, remembering all the times that Truckman has had your back in the past. "Okay," you finally reply. "I trust you."

36

You feel the Trucker's code tugging at your heartstrings and pushing you onward. You didn't ask to be thrust into this situation, but you've made a commitment to the journey. Once a truck leaves the warehouse, you'll get it to its destination if it's the last thing you do.

This is your last ride, anyway. You might as well make it count.

"I've got this," you finally continue.

"Thanks," Truckman offers. "Keep in touch."

The call ends and you're plunged into the quiet of the road once more. It takes a while longer for you to fully center yourself, but eventually things pull back together.

You consider turning on some music, but before you move on completely, you consider one last thing, a curious idea that hangs coyly at the back of your mind.

Truckman refused to tell you what important artifact you're actually carrying, and with sound reason. Still, you can't help but consider going back there and seeing if you can find the secret compartment for yourself.

Pull over and search the truck on page 72
Keep driving on page 76

You take a moment to size up the figure, considering all the evidence before you and then finally making your call.

"That's a slashman," you announce.

The sentient potato smiles and nods. "You're absolutely correct. If that was a hockey player, he'd be wet from the ice and that water dripping off of him would be cold. The water is lukewarm, so he's definitely a slashman."

The large, masked figure is almost out the door at this point, pushing through and causing the bell to jingle as he makes his exit. With a split second to spare, the potato calls out from behind, stopping him in his tracks.

"Hey!" the sentient vegetable yells, "would you mind settling a bet for us?"

The masked dinosaur slowly turns around, his vacant eyes staring into you as he continues to drip onto the tile floor below. "Sure" he finally offers, the single word falling out of his throat with a deep thud.

"Are you a hockey player or a slashman?" the potato questions.

The massive figure hesitates for a moment, his breathing heavy against his mask as you wait intently for his response.

"I'm a slashman," the dinosaur finally reveals, "but it's my day off. Have a good one."

With that, the figure turns around and heads out the door, trudging onward and disappearing from sight.

You glance back at the sentient potato, impressed with her observational skills, but also quite thrilled with your own.

"You won," the living vegetable reminds you. "You can pick from anything up here at the counter."

Excited, your eyes begin to dart around at the various options. There's all kinds of candy and small trinkets laying around, but two particular items catch your eye.

The first is a stick of bubblegum, which isn't all that special other than the fact you've been craving a good stick of gum to pass the time on your drive.

Next is a lucky keychain that hangs from a small display hook nearby, glinting under the florescent gas station lights as it rocks ever so

38

subtly from side to side. The keychain has a small, lucky unicorn shoe dangling from the end of it.

Take the lucky unicorn shoe on page 110
Take the bubblegum on page 95

You wake up slowly, the first hints of morning sunlight dancing across your eyelids and gradually pulling you out of a deep, deep slumber. You must have passed out quick, but you can feel in your bones that this rest was exactly what you needed.

You sit up, stretching and yawning as you allow yourself a peaceful moment. Your bag is sitting right next to you, exactly where it should be, and The Big Red Button is still tucked safely within.

You climb to your feet and spend the next short while getting ready, then eventually make your way out into the parking lot.

Suddenly, the relative calm of the morning comes to an abrupt end. You notice that your truck has been booted with some kind of magical device, the strange object latched around your front wheel to keep you from leaving.

"What the hell?" you groan, approaching your vehicle in a state of frustration.

As you draw closer you notice that a business card has been tucked under the windshield wiper, and you climb up to pull it off.

"Bazara's Junkyard And Salvage," you read aloud, turning the card over in your hands. There's no phone number listed, but the address just happens to be a short walk down the road from your motel.

Hoping to get this sorted out quickly, you being the trek, making your way along the side of this empty road as the sounds of the early morning fill your ears. You're certainly frustrated, but this is clearly just some kind of big misunderstanding and it shouldn't take long to get you back on the highway with the radio cranked and the windows down.

As you walk onward, you're treated to an absolutely majestic sunrise, the orange glowing orb making its ascent with utter grace and bathing your journey in warm light. Your shadow stretches long across the landscape, and you enjoy watching it shorten as you continue along.

Eventually, you find yourself at an old junkyard that matches the address you're looking for. This place would be fascinating regardless of your quest, all kinds of scraps piled up in awkward creations, forming walls and tunnels like some kind of bizarre medieval lair.

"Hello?" you call out, but there's no response.

You begin to wander deeper into the junkyard until, eventually, you hear a soft purr and catch sight of a sentient motorcycle rumbling up to you. She has long dark hair and a kind smile.

"I'm Bazara," the motorcycle offers. "Can I help you?"

"Yeah," you reply, trying your best to not sound annoyed but having a difficult time. "I woke up this morning to find there was a boot on my car."

You hand over the card and the sentient motorcycle takes it, nodding in confirmation. "Over at the old motel?"

"Yep," you reply.

"We got a call you were illegally parked," she explains. "Didn't want to give you the full tow, so I thought this would be better."

"Illegally parked?" you blurt. "Says who? I was a guest at that hotel."

Bazara nods along, her expression one of care and understanding. "Well, there must be a mistake then," she offers. "Come on back to the shack and we'll get this sorted out."

The living bike revs her engine and then rumbles off into the junkyard, heading into the maze as you follow behind.

"I'm really sorry about that," Bazara calls back over her shoulder. "These things happen sometimes."

You eventually arrive at an old shack with a large sign on top reading, predictably, 'Bazara's Junkyard And Salvage.' The motorcycle rolls up to the door and pushes inside.

You enter behind her to find a strange little room absolutely covered in American flags and other patriotic paraphernalia. It's a stunning display, and the icing on the cake is an enormous bald eagle that sits in the corner, surrounded by a metal cage and staring daggers into you.

There's a counter with a cash register, and behind that is a back room.

"Wait here," Bazara says. "Well get this sorted."

You do as you're told as the living motorcycle rumbles off into her private quarters, closing the door slightly behind her so that only a small sliver remains open.

The eagle watches you closely as you make your way around the shelves, picking up various products and looking them over curiously. Eventually, an item behind the counter catches your eye.

There are a few of these small containers stacked in a pile. The top of the tin reads 'Bazara's Boot Buster: Guaranteed To Undo Most Magical Automotive Boots."

"It's definitely their truck," comes the voice of the motorcycle, faintly drifting out from the back room.

Your heart skips a beat as you hear this. You lean out a bit to get a good view of Bazara through the crack in the door. She's on her phone.

"Do you want me to cast a lock spell and keep them occupied until you get here?" Bazara continues. "Yes. They have a bag with them. I'm guessing the device is inside."

You're in deep trouble, and you have to act fast if you wanna get out of here with The Big Red Button still in your possession.

The way you see it, there are two options, and both involve running as fast as you can.

Unleash the eagle as a distraction and get out of there on page 173
Grab Bazara's Boot Buster and get out of there on page 55

You veer off toward the casino garden and soon enough the blackjack and craps tables give way to a lush, towering atrium of flowers and vines. This area is much calmer and quieter than the rest of The Grand Buckaroo Hotel And Casino, complete with soft, breezy music and the soothing sound of a small waterfall as it trickles across the false rockface nearby.

You slow down, then creep up off of the main path, slipping behind one of the many enormous floral arrangements that are positioned throughout the room. You freeze right here, holding your breath as you listen closely for the unicorn security team.

It's not long before they come running through the indoor garden, the gang slowing down their footsteps and then splitting off in various directions.

You close your eyes tight, your heart slamming within your chest as you maintain your stillness as carefully as possible.

"Anything over there?" one of the unicorns calls out.

"Nothing here," another one of the creatures replies from his side of the garden.

"I think I might have something," another one of them chimes in, this unicorn's voice emerging from alarmingly close to your hiding spot. "You see this? The flowers are broken in a trail that leads up over here."

You realize now that it's only a matter of time before they discover your hiding spot. Not wanting to wait around until they're standing right behind you, you immediately spring into action and start running again, traipsing through the colorful flowers as the unicorns begin to scream and shout. You've almost made it out of the flowerbed when one of the security guards leaps through the air and tackles you to the ground in a plume of brilliant orange petals.

Soon enough, all the unicorns are upon you. They roughly pull you to your feet and then drag you through the garden as the casino patrons nearby look on in horror and confusion.

"I didn't do it!" you cry out. "It's not me! I swear!"

Soon enough, you're approaching an inconspicuous door that likely brings you to an employee's only area of the building. The unicorns don't even open the door for you, just slam you through it and keep going.

"Hey! What the hell?" you blurt, now finding yourself in a sterile white hallway the runs the length of the structure.

The squad of unicorns barely pay you a second glance, just continue onward through a maze of hallways and then eventually down some stairs into the belly of the casino. No matter how much you struggle you simply can't break away from the group.

You approach another door and the unicorns throw you through it, following behind as you collapse to the ground. You're significantly roughed up now, and as you struggle to collect your senses you hear a terrifyingly familiar voice drift across your ears.

"Hello there," Ted hisses, the bright red devil sitting in a chair before you. "I see you've brought me The Big Red Button. How kind of you."

The unicorns grab your bag and tear it away, then hand it over to the devil.

Ted pulls out the device and turns it over in his clawed hands, inspecting it with a mischievous smile that grows wider and wider by the second.

"Don't," is all you can think to say. "You can't."

"Oh, but I can," Ted retorts. "Cobbler Enterprises is much more than just a shipping and cargo business. Sure, it started simple enough with Cobbler Trucking, but since then we've moved into media, politics... hell, we've even gotten into the casino industry."

The unicorns all start to laugh as you watch in horror. Ted stands up from his table and strolls past you with a wink, waving goodbye with The Big Red Button in his hands. The unicorns follow behind, pushing you back as you make one final attempt to escape.

The next thing you know, the door is closing and locking you in. You pound your fists as hard as you can against the metal but it's no use. There isn't even cell phone service down here.

Eventually, you end up turning and sliding down the wall in agony. You wait like this for a long, long time, so long that you barely even notice when the fabric of reality begins to split apart.

THE END

44

After giving it some thought, you finally decide to pull over on the side of the road and allow yourself a minute to rest. There's a great sense of relief as your tires crunch over the gravel beneath, and the second you put your rig in park and turn the keys, you realize what a good idea this little pause really was.

You close your eyes, allowing the relaxation to flow through you like a cool and gentle river. It's hard to tell how long you stay like this, but by the time you open your eyes again the sun has disappeared completely, revealing a glorious, star filled sky above.

You see now that your headlights are shining directly at a small wooden sign, a marker so inconspicuous you would've never even noticed it without stopping.

"Home of Truth, Utah," you read aloud. "Population zero."

The sign is especially curious since there are no structures to be found in the immediate vicinity, abandoned or otherwise. You do, however, notice a faint, ghostly light off in the distance. It's hard to tell exactly what it is, but it appears to be emanating from somewhere in the middle of this grassy field.

You're curious, but also a little frightened.

Investigate the light on page 128
Keep driving on page 53

As much as you'd like to pull off an extra task before making your escape, the longer you stick around, the more dangerous it becomes. Your mission right now is survival, and that means hitting the road before they have a chance to get in your way.

You ready yourself for action, taking a brief moment and then turning the keys and starting up your rig. As the truck roars to life your headlights erupt out across the field of long grass before you, revealing the startled, bright red face of Ted plastered with a look of absolute shock. He immediately points a long, clawed finger toward you, attempting to cast some kind of spell, but you're just too far away for his dark magic to work.

Your truck peels out, spitting gravel everywhere before catching and lurching forward. Soon enough, your flying down the dark highway, tearing through the night as you nervously glance in your rearview mirror.

It takes a while for the two silhouetted figures to return to their cab, but eventually Ted's enormous black and red truck roars to life. The devil slams on the gas and soon enough he's rumbling right behind you, pushing the limits of his vehicle in an effort to catch up.

"Oh shit, oh shit," you start repeating to yourself, drumming your fingers on the steering wheel as Ted creeps closer and closer.

The truck behind you blares its menacing horn, the sound echoing out across the landscape like some enormous creaking gate of heck. To your horror, you quickly realize that Ted's maximum speed is more than enough to overtake you, and soon the giant truck is pulling up right alongside.

You glance over to see the one-eyed bigfoot is, in fact, the driver, while Ted sits in the passenger seat. The devil smiles wide, his window down as he climbs halfway out of the vehicle. He begins to chant some kind of magic incantation, brilliant green energy swirling around his hands. Moments later, Ted thrusts his claws toward you, a swirling mist erupting forth and somehow finding its way into the cab of your truck.

You begin to feel yourself losing control of the truck almost instantly, and when you attempt to correct course this proves to be even more difficult. You glance down to see that your hands and arms are shrinking, transforming into something scaly and inhuman. You cry out in terror, but the sound of your voice quickly morphs into a strangled hiss. It's only then that you realize you're turning into a snake.

The truck begins to slow as your foot leaves the gas pedal, but

46

you've already gained enough momentum that it doesn't have much effect. As you slither across the seat of your truck cabin, you can feel the weight of the vehicle shift, drifting ever so slightly and then finally making a sharp turn to the right. The truck rattles loudly, and although you can't see out of the window, you can sense that you've steered off a sharp embankment.

Suddenly, there's a loud crash, the whole world turning upside-down as you're thrown into the air. You catch a brief glimpse through the windshield of an enormous rock, but you're not sure if that's a boulder in your path or the ground rushing up toward you after jumping a cliff.

You don't have much time to consider either option, because the last thing you hear is the deafening crunch of metal on impact.

THE END

After giving it some thought, you finally decide to pull over on the side of the road and allow yourself a minute to rest. There's a great sense of relief as your tires crunch over the gravel beneath, and the second you put your rig in park and turn the keys, you realize what a good idea this little pause really was.

You close your eyes, allowing the relaxation to flow through you like a cool and gentle river. It's hard to tell how long you stay like this, but by the time you open your eyes again the sun has disappeared completely, revealing a glorious, star filled sky above.

You see now that your headlights are shining directly at a small wooden sign, a marker so inconspicuous you would've never even noticed it without stopping.

"Home of Truth, Utah," you read aloud. "Population zero."

The sign is especially curious since there are no structures to be found in the immediate vicinity, abandoned or otherwise. You do, however, notice a faint, ghostly light off in the distance. It's hard to tell exactly what it is, but it appears to be emanating from somewhere in the middle of this grassy field.

You're curious, but also a little frightened.

Investigate the light on page 6
Keep driving on page 62

Seizing the moment, you keep your head low and rush through the grass toward the road, avoiding their line of sight as you sneak over to the cab of their truck. This vehicle, courtesy of Cobbler Trucking, has been left unlocked, and you gasp excitedly as you find that the keys have been carelessly left in the ignition. You swiftly pull out the DEVIL KEYS and put them in your pocket.

The headlights immediately shut off, which has most certainly alerted Ted and his bigfoot companion.

"Hey!" the devil cries out from the darkness in confusion.

Your eyes on the prize, you hurry back over to your own vehicle and climb into the driver's seat. Once there, you waste no time starting it up with a loud roar.

As your headlights illuminate the grass before you, you see Ted with a look of absolute shock plastered across his face. He immediately points a long, clawed finger at you, attempting to cast some kind of a spell, but you're just too far away at this point and his dark magic doesn't work.

You start to laugh, then honk twice as you haul off down the road, literally leaving these two criminals in the dust as you continue on your way. Watching in the rearview mirror, you see them climb into their truck and then start yelling wildly, upset to discover that their keys are missing.

You drive like mad, not satisfied with pulling over until you've put as many miles between you and the other truck as possible. Eventually, however, the pounding of your heart begins to subside. You remind yourself that you don't need to keep glancing in the rearview mirror, and that Ted is still somewhere far, far behind you.

Hoping for an explanation in this chaos, you decide to call Truckman.

The phone barely rings once before your boss picks up, his familiar voice sounding out through your speakers. "What's up?" he questions.

"I was about to ask you the same thing!" you blurt. "I just got attacked by a devil and a bigfoot from Cobbler Trucking. They want the device but they couldn't find it."

Truckman lets out a long sigh, as though his deepest fears are coming true before his very eyes. "Are you okay?" he questions.

"Yeah," you reply, "but barely."

"I'm sorry to bring you into this," Truckman continues, "but you're the only one I trusted on this job. The device you're carrying is called The

Big Red Button. Whoever pushes the button will be sent to another timeline that is slightly more full of love."

"Sounds pretty nice right about now," you admit.

"It does," Truckman retorts, "but *you* can't push it. At least, not yet. You need to stick around in this layer of reality to make sure your package gets to San Diego in one piece. There's a scientist there who will use The Big Red Button to prove even more love, but if the device falls into the wrong hands it could be reverse engineered into something terrible. It could tear apart the fabric of this very timeline."

You nod along to these words, fully understanding your mission. You have no intention of letting The Big Red Button fall into Ted's hands, especially not on your last ride as a trucker.

"You can count on me, boss," you assume Truckman.

"I know," he replies. "Now that they know you've got it in the truck, you should take The Big Red Button out of the secret compartment and keep it on you at all times. The magic lock is simple enough, just got back there and knock three times, then say 'love is real.'"

"That's it?" you retort.

"That's it," Truckman continues. "Devils have a really hard time with that last phrase."

You say your goodbyes and hang up, continuing on into the night with a newly renewed sense of purpose. You make sure to turn off the main drag a bit before finding your motel for the evening.

When you finally pull into the parking lot you're absolutely exhausted. Still, there's one thing left to do.

You exit the cab and head around to the back of your truck, then climb up into the cargo hold. It's completely empty, and the idea of a secret compartment hidden somewhere within these four flat, blank walls is hard to believe.

You take a deep breath and let it out, then knock three times on the side of your truck with your hand. "Love is real," you state confidently.

Nothing happens.

Your brow furrowed, you try this process again, this time moving over to the other side of the refrigerated chamber. You knock once more and say the magic words, yet your results are the same.

Growing worried, you decide to give it one last go. This time, you rap your heel against the floor of the truck.

"Love is real," you say aloud.

Suddenly, there's a loud clang as a panel slides up and over, magical energy wafting up from within this tiny hidden area. You bend down and carefully withdraw a small box, covered in wires and sporting an enormous red button on the top. You carefully place it in your bag, then climb down from the back of the truck and close it up.

Until you reach San Diego, this bag isn't leaving your side.

Rest at the motel on page 39

"There's gotta be another way," you offer. "Show me that scan of the building again."

Riley pulls up the holographic display, which floats in the air before you as you carefully inspect the layout of the warehouse. You're looking specifically at the area where the real Borson Reems is being held.

"That's just a thin wall to the outside, right?" you question, pointing to the backside of the closet. "Do you have a way to get in there without drawing attention?"

"I've got just the thing," Riley replies.

The car suddenly goes quiet, entering stealth mode as the purr of the engine disappears completely. You begin to roll forward, making your way around to the side of the building where Ted's big-rig is parked. You continue past the truck and eventually until up facing a very specific point on the wall of warehouse.

Riley's hood pops open and a small mechanical arm emerges. A brilliant red light begins to shine at the wall in the form of a pencil-thin laser beam, moving slowly across the surface in a gradual, circular motion. Heat and smoke begin to rise up as the laser cuts a hole, eventually completing the circle.

Now it's your turn for action. You climb out of the driver's seat and approach the round cutout, gripping the edge and then, ever so carefully, pulling it back. Soon enough, this metallic circle is popping out of the wall. You brace yourself for the weight, then lower it down slowly to the ground and reveal an enormous hole.

Behind the wall is Borson Reems, *the real Borson Reems,* strapped to a chair with rope and gagged with a cloth. His eyes go wide when he sees you, at first a little frightened and then transitioning to excitement when he realizes what's happening.

You quickly untie the scientist and help him to his feet, then make your way back out through the hole.

"Let's roll," you offer to Borson Reems as you climb into your billion dollar sportscar, closing the gull-wing doors and revving the engine. You make a squealing U-turn and head back up the street with a wide grin on your face.

Confidently, you reach into your bag, which sits on the backseat, and pull out The Big Red Button. You hand it over to Borson.

"Here's your package," you offer, closing the book on your final delivery.

You drive off as the sun continues to rise on a brand new day, excited to see what comes next in a world with just a little bit more love.

THE END

As intriguing as this mysterious light is, you've got an important task at hand and any amount of distraction is just not worth it. Besides, it hard to imagine what kind of good could ever come from roaming the open plains of the Utah wilds in search of some strange phantom illumination.

Better to keep your focus on the mission than get lost in the dark on the way.

You put your truck in drive and pull out onto the open road once more, feeling the slightest bit rejuvenated from your momentary break. It's enough to keep your head on straight just a little while longer and put some miles under your belt.

Suddenly, your headlights reveal a tire strip laid out across the road before you, a long thin row of spikes that are specifically designed to pierce the rubber of your tires.

There's a loud, earsplitting bang and now the truck is losing control, shuddering with terrifying power as you struggle to maintain a straight path along the empty highway. You can feel the back of your rig fishtailing side to side, and for a moment you get a sense that the whole thing is going to tip right over.

Fortunately, this doesn't happen. Soon enough, you're pulling off onto the side of the road and slowing to a stop, the flap of a ragged tire sounding loud in your ear.

You open up the door to your cab and leap down onto the gravel to assess the damage. Your truck is built to withstand a lot, and fortunately the strip only managed to puncture one of your tires. Still, that's more than enough to keep you from going anywhere for the time being.

Even more pressing, however, is the terrifying question that repeats itself over and over again in your head, a warning alarm at the forefront of your mind.

Who laid the tire strip?

Without warning, a pair of headlights slice through the darkness before you. The red and black semi-truck from Cobbler Trucking reveals its enormous and terrifying shape, parked on the side of the road just a few yards away. The vehicle begins to slowly creep toward you.

Run off into the fields and hide on page 169
Stay and confront them on page 188

54

Instead of aggression, you decide to come at things with a different approach.

"Whatever you're looking for, you're not gonna find it," you offer. "It's just chocolate milk back there."

Ted is skeptical of your words, but for a brief moment you actually see an expression of doubt flicker across his face.

Eventually, the one-eyed bigfoot finishes emptying out your truck and covering the asphalt with shattered glass and chocolate milk. He returns to you and the devil, announcing his findings.

"Just milk back there," he states bluntly.

Ted hesitates for a moment, not wanting to accept this announcement and then finally succumbing to his anger.

"Shit!" the bright red devil screams, punching the side of your vehicle. "This must be the wrong truck!"

"What should we do?" the bigfoot questions.

"We should get out there and find it," Ted continues, already turning around and marching back to his rig. The bigfoot and the devil climb up into their cab and soon enough they're taking off, pulling back onto the road and roaring into the dark night from which they came.

When they're finally gone you let out a long sigh of relief, then tension within your body finally dissipating. A crisis was averted, at least for now, but soon enough they're going to realize they had it right the first time and come back looking for you.

You better be gone by then.

If you have the spare truck tire turn to page 70
If you don't have the spare truck tire turn to page 126

You leap over the counter and grab the tin of MAGIC BOOT CREAM, then jump back over and run as fast as you can toward the door. You slam into it and keep barreling onward, sprinting out into the junkyard and not looking back.

You can hear a commotion behind you, the eagle screeching and Bazara revving her engine, but you've still got a hell of a lead on them as you begin to weave in and out of the cars and scrap metal. You've entered the maze, and while they certainly know this place better than you do, at least you've been presented with a few options for where to hide.

There's no question the motorcycle and bird are faster than you are, but maybe if you keep your wits about you, you might be able to outmaneuver them.

Continuing onward, you suddenly find yourself faced with a fork in the maze. Either side looks like just another tunnel through these towering stacks of cars, with no indication of what lies ahead.

You'll just have to take your chances.

Head to the left on page 82
Head to the right on page 105

"I'm sorry," you insist. "As fun as it sounds, I've gotta stay focused right now."

Michelle shrugs, finally accepting your response. "Hey, Blackjack's not for everyone."

Soon enough, you and the sentient corn are driving down the Las Vegas Strip, headed toward Michelle's destination at The Grand Buckaroo Hotel And Casino. Once there, the two of you will part ways, but until then you sit back and enjoy the brilliant flashing lights of this truly unique city.

Your gaze jumps from one side of the street to the other as you take it all in, appreciating the glitz and the glamor of this desert town built on hard luck and good fun.

It's not long before you see the brilliant glittering neon of The Grand Buckaroo, this behemoth hotel towering above you with its notorious waving cowboy all lit up in yellow and orange. Michelle pulls into the parking structure, which winds in and out of the building and eventually leads you deep down into the depths of the casino. They do this, of course, so that even if you don't want to gamble you're still forced to walk across the casino floor on your way outside.

No matter, your mind is razor sharp and focused on the task ahead. Your next job is finding some new means of transportation, which shouldn't be that hard out on the strip.

Michelle eventually pulls into her parking spot and the two of you climb out, hugging warmly after getting to know each other quite well during the course of your trip.

"Good luck," you offer with deep sincerity. "I believe in you."

"Likewise," the living vegetable replies with a wink. "You'll be in San Diego before you know it."

You share an elevator ride to the casino floor and then finally part ways for good, each one of you taking off in the opposite direction.

Soon enough, you find yourself totally alone as you wander through The Grand Buckaroo Hotel And Casino, struggling to find an exit and falling prey to their intentionally confusing architecture. The casino wants you to get lost, because the longer you spend wandering around in here, the more likely you are to play.

"Hey! Stop right there!" comes a gruff voice, suddenly cutting through the chaotic sound of stacking chips and ringing bells.

You turn around to see a group of five unicorns in black suits walking toward you. They all wear dark sunglasses, despite the fact that you're currently indoors, and have stern looks plastered across their faces.

The leader of the bunch, who sports a particularly unique light green coloration, steps forward. "You're coming with us," he commands.

"Wait, what?" you blurt, utterly confused. "Why?"

"You've been caught running a scam on the security cameras," the lead unicorn continues.

"I literally just got here," you blurt. "There's been a mistake."

"Well, come with us and we can clear things up," the unicorn continues as his friends surround you.

Run away to page 67
Go with the unicorns to page 151

58

You shake your head from side to side, rattling out the cobwebs and refocusing your effort on the task at hand. You need to get The Big Red Button to San Diego, and the sooner you can accomplish this task the better. While Las Vegas is a fantastic place to take a vacation, you'd rather skip it for the sake of putting a few more road hours under your belt.

Unfortunately, the second getting a little sleep even remotely crosses your mind you find an unstoppable yawn creeping up and sneaking its way out of your throat.

You'll call it a night soon enough, maybe at one of these little desert towns just a few hours onward, but not yet.

Soon enough, the lights of Las Vegas are fading into the distance while the vast darkness of the wide open desert stretches on before you.

You turn up the radio, cranking the music to keep yourself awake. Every time you feel yourself nodding off you give your head another firm shake, even slapping your cheeks in an attempt to hold yourself together. Unfortunately, there's something hypnotic about watching the endless weave of the yellow and white lines, pulling you farther and farther away from your conscious mind and coaxing you into a dangerous trancelike state.

Eventually, the weight of your eyelids is just too powerful to hold back any longer.

The first thing you notice is how beautiful the sunrise is, which is strange considering the fact that you're hanging upside down and sideways, scrunched up against the metal interior of your truck cab like a discarded rag doll.

When you realize where you are and what has happened you gasp aloud, frantically struggling to untangle yourself from the seatbelt. You manage to find the clasp and pop it open, dropping to the wall, which is now the floor, with a loud thud. There's glass everywhere, but the kind that's specifically developed to create safe, tiny beads when it shatters. With this in mind, you crawl forward a bit, edging toward the sunlight and then finally freeing yourself from the wreckage.

You turn around to find that your suspicions are correct. You'd fallen asleep behind the wheel and ended up careening out into the open desert, traveling so far away that no other motorists could catch a glimpse of the wreckage and report it. In fact, you can't even see the freeway from here, discovering nothing but a strange dirt track that seems to extend across the sand for miles and miles, until finally hitting the wrong slope and tipping your vehicle onto its side.

"Well... damn," is all you can think to say, just staring at the wreckage and wishing you'd taken a break to rest your eyes back in Vegas.

Suddenly, you remember the device. You immediately spring into action, frantically searching around in the remains of the cabin for your bag and The Big Red Button that's held within.

The second you find it, a powerful wave of relief washes over you. The truck may be useless, but the journey's not over yet.

With nothing left to do here in the wreckage, you decide to begin your journey back to the main road, retracing these haphazard dirt tracks from the evening before.

Strangely, the farther you walk, the more these tracks begin to muddle with those of other off-road vehicles. It becomes so bad that you lose grip on which truck you're actually following, and quickly realize that, at this point, you might not even be heading toward the freeway at all.

As the sun continues to rise, the air becomes hotter and hotter. You hadn't really considered this a problem, but the longer you spend out here in the middle of nowhere, the more parched your throat becomes. You're starting to get desperate when you suddenly notice an utterly bizarre sight emerging in the distance.

You approach and find yourself greeted by a small tollbooth-like structure, featuring a gated entrance and fifteen or twenty different cameras pointed down at you from a pole above. Beyond this gate is nothing but even more open desert.

The most alarming thing, however, is a plaque on the booth that reads in simple, block letters 'Area 52'.

"Hands up!" someone calls out gruffly, suddenly emerging from the booth in a bright silver uniform that strongly resembles a space suit.

The guard is a yellowish green triceratops. He's holding a futuristic weapon that sparks and dances with a strange red light, a humming laser beam just aching to be fired off in my direction.

Run away on page 138
Freeze and follow orders on page 134

60

There are plenty of things about this stegosaurus that rub you the wrong way, but none of them are important enough to keep you from declining his help in such a dire situation. A request for your one and only spare tire, however, is simply a bridge too far.

"Actually, I'll just take care of it myself," you state.

"You sure about that?" the dinosaur questions.

You nod confidently, then turn around and head back out the door of his gas station.

The cold air tingles your face as you carefully make your way back down the hill, this time even more focused on maintaining your footing. Fortunately, you somehow manage to creep back down to the crash site without falling on your ass.

You take a moment to assess the situation and then maneuver yourself around to the front of the truck. It's a large vehicle, but you have no problem getting in there by popping the hood and climbing up onto the front bumper.

From here, you're provided a clear view down into the belly of the beast, immediately noticing that your brake lines have, in fact, been severed. Strangely, it's not a clear cut like you might've expected, but a ragged slice from someone rubbing a hard, pointed spear back and forth across the wire.

"Turn around slowly," comes a strange, high-pitched voice from behind you. It has a bizarre, sing-song cadence, creating an almost gurgling quality.

You do as you're told, turning around slowly to find that you're surrounded by six enormous jackalopes. While you've never seen a jackalope before in real life, you're heard plenty of stories about these huge rabbits with sharp antlers protruding from the top of their heads.

While some claim this society of wild creatures is mischievous and fun, other's describe their actions as downright criminal. It looks like the latter were right.

"Open up the back of the truck," the head jackalope demands, the spikes of his enormous antlers shining bright and pointy.

"No," you reply.

"Open the back of the truck," the creature gurgles again, this time with much more force. The group of jackalopes hop a little closer, closing in their circle around you.

"I've got a delivery to make," you state bluntly. "I'm not letting anyone into the back of my rig."

You can tell by the looks on the faces of these creatures that this kind of refusal is not something they're used to. They're both surprised and slightly amused at the gall on display.

The lead jackalope takes one final step toward you, rearing up on his hind legs so that the already enormous rabbit can look you dead in the eyes.

"We're not violent by nature," the creature explains, "but we do what we have to do. The cold months out here can be ruthless, and a pack needs food to eat and milk to drink."

"I can't let you in there," you repeat, trembling now.

"These horns are sharp," the creature continues. "Don't make us use them."

With every passing second, it's becoming clearer and clearer just how limited your options are. If you don't allow them into the cargo you're hauling, then you'll end up fighting the whole pack.

Glancing around at the group of vicious jackalopes, you're not quite sure if you can take them.

Open the cargo hold on page 171
Fight the jackalopes on page 94

It takes a hearty amount of mental fortitude, but you somehow manage to pull yourself together and focus on the task at hand. Maybe it's the mission itself that keeps you in line, a singular goal to maintain while everything else swirls past; a lighthouse in the storm.

You plow ahead as the sun disappears completely, but only a few miles have passed when disaster strikes.

Without warning, your headlights reveal a tire strip laid out across the road before you, a long thin row of spikes that are specifically designed to pierce the rubber of your tires.

There's a loud, earsplitting bang and now the truck is losing control, shuddering with terrifying power as you struggle to maintain a straight path along the empty highway. You can feel the back of your rig fishtailing from side to side, and for a moment you get a sense the whole thing is going to tip right over.

Fortunately, this doesn't happen.

Soon enough, you're pulling off onto the side of the road and slowing to a stop, the flap of a ragged tire sounding loud in your ear.

You open up the door to your cab and leap down onto the gravel to assess the damage. Your truck is built to withstand a lot, and the strip only managed to puncture one of your tires. Still, that's more than enough damage to keep you from going anywhere for the time being.

Even more pressing, however, is the terrifying question that repeats itself over and over again in your head, a warning alarm at the forefront of your mind. Who laid this trap?

Without warning, a pair of headlights slice through the darkness before you. The red and black Cobbler Trucking big-rig reveals its enormous and terrifying shape, parked on the side of the road just a few yards away. The vehicle begins to slowly creep forward.

Run and hide in the field on page 163
Stay and confront them on page 194

This whole episode has been going on long enough. It's time to admit that you need a little help and take the dinosaur up on his offer.

"Okay, sure," you finally reply, nodding in acceptance. "You've got yourself a deal."

"Get the spare and I'll get started," replies the stegosaurus.

You turn and climb up into the cab of your truck, moving a few things around and then finally pulling forth this highly coveted spare truck tire. It's heavy, but you manage to pull it out and drop it onto the ground with a satisfying, rubbery thud.

The dinosaur is nowhere to be found.

"Hey!" you call out. "I got your tire!"

Suddenly, you gasp as the stegosaurus appears beside you. He's folding up a hunting knife and putting it in his pocket. Once that's done, he hands you a small, fuzzy item.

"A LUCKY JACKALOPE'S FOOT," he explains.

You glance over the stegosaurus's shoulder at the body of the jackalope, then back at the dinosaur. He nods.

"Uh... thanks," you finally reply, then hand over his item to complete the exchange. "Here's your *SPARE TRUCK TIRE*."

Now that the technicalities have been settled, the dinosaur gets to work. He strolls over to your truck and pops the hood, then begins to rummage around on the inside. He's got a rather small selection of tools with him, but they seem to be getting the job done.

Moments later, the dinosaur drops down and wipes his hands confidently. "That should do it," he offers.

"All fixed?" you cry out with excitement.

"All fixed," the dinosaur confirms, then turns and starts making his way back up the hill.

You climb back up into the driver's seat and start your engine, smiling wide as it roars to life with a familiar purr.

While other vehicles might be completely trapped in this situation, your truck is built for power. It takes a minute, but eventually you manage to back yourself up out of the ditch and return to the asphalt.

Soon enough, you're off and running once again, making your way down the winding road ahead.

Continue into Utah on page 97

Why the hell not?

Instead of heading up to the room, you make your way out onto the casino floor, hunting through the mess of slot machines and craps tables until you eventually find yourself at a check-in booth for The World Series Of Blackjack.

You hand your card over to the woman behind the counter. "I'd like to enter," you state proudly.

"Wonderful!" she replies. "We're just getting started. Perfect timing!"

The woman at the desk takes your coupon and prints out a ticket in exchange, handing it over to you. The slip features a randomly generated seat assignment at one of the various blackjack tables.

"Good luck," the woman offers.

Soon enough, you find yourself wandering over to an empty seat. You double check this is the correct spot, still feeling incredibly nervous but trying your best to stay cool, then sit down like you know what you're doing.

You give the other four players at this small table a nod.

"I'm Keith," says the player right next to you, a sentient jet plane with a handsome face and a wide smile. He extends a wing and you shake it firmly. "Nice to meet you."

"You too," you offer in return. "How's it going so far?"

Keith shrugs. "Competition just stared, but I'm feeling good."

The sentient vehicle gestures toward the stack of chips in front of him, which is significantly more than the rest of the players around you.

"Whoa," you blurt. "How'd you manage that."

"Well, I'm a pretty good card counter," Keith admits.

Your eyes go wide as you glance over at the dealer, shocked the jet plane would just reveal this out loud.

The dealer doesn't react.

"It's not illegal," Keith informs you, "Just discouraged. For these competitions, however, The Grand Buckaroo Casino says that card counting is fair game."

"Oh, whoa," you reply. "I didn't know that."

"That's not even my real secret weapon," Keith admits.

You lean in a little closer, hoping this friendly, sentient plane will offer you a bit of his wisdom. "What is?" you question.

"I just play with love," Keith continues. "If I get in a bad mood then I know it's time to leave. As long as I'm playing with love, I tend to do pretty well."

"I'll give it a try," you reply.

"Good," Keith offers with a smile. "Because you're up."

"Oh!" you blurt, glancing back at the two cards sitting before you.

The dealer stares at you with a devastatingly expressionless face. "Would you like to hit or stand?" they ask.

Your blackjack knowledge suddenly flashes before your eyes, a split second refresher on how to play that's there and gone before you even have a chance to acknowledge it.

"Uh... hit," you reply.

The dealer lays down another card, bringing your total to twenty one. That's a good thing.

"Nice work," the jet plane leans over to whisper in your year. "You're gonna do just fine."

You continue playing throughout the evening, trusting your instincts and trying your best to remember Keith's advice about playing with love in your heart. Eventually, the other players begin to lose all of their chips and slip away, while the stacks belonging to you and your new jet plane friend grow steadily larger.

Soon enough, the dealers take a break and your chips are all collected, then moved over to the final table.

You have five minutes to grab a snack or stretch your legs, and during this time another player, who happens to be a sentient corn on the cob, approaches you.

"How you doing?" she asks.

"Pretty good, actually," you retort, surprising even yourself. "I made it to the final table."

The living vegetable's eyes go wide. You can tell that she's sincerely impressed and happy for you. "Really? That's great!"

You nod. "How about yourself?"

The corn shakes her head in disappointment. "Just wasn't my night," she opines. "I got knocked out just before the break. I guess that's the way these competitions go when you close in on the final table, if you don't have a little luck on your side then you're dead in the water."

Suddenly, a bell rings, alerting you that the competition will begin again in thirty seconds.

"You better get back there," the living corn reminds you.

If you have a lucky jackalope's foot turn to page 115
If you have a lucky unicorn shoe turn to page 158
If you have no lucky items turn to page 153

Without a word you spring into action, turning as fast as you can and then breaking out into a sprint in the exact opposite direction. You didn't exactly plan for this kind of escape, so you immediately find yourself ducking and dodging through the crowd behind you, nearly bowling over a waitress who just barely maintains the balance of her chocolate milk tray.

Soon enough, you're high tailing it through the ringing, chattering casino floor, the flashing slot machines whipping by on either side while the unicorns follow in hot pursuit. You glance back over your shoulder to see a few of them splitting off in either direction, likely attempting to block the exits.

That just means you'll need to kick up the speed a little more.

"Get back here!" the lead security unicorn demands, calling out and shaking his fist in anger.

Your pursuers have a distinct advantage in knowing the layout here, but you manage to catch a glimpse of some hanging signs as they pass you by.

To your left is the casino garden, and to the right is the pool.

Head for the garden on page 42
Head for the pool on page 165

68

There's something about this moment you just don't like. Maybe it's the fact that you've already had to deal with so much danger and suspense already, and now you just don't want to risk it.

Maybe the sentient living corn is just too nice, suspiciously available to provide a ride in exactly the same direction you're headed.

Either way, you decide to decline.

"I'm fine," you reply. "Thanks for the offer."

The living corn looks up the road, then back behind her, taking note of just how far out in the middle of nowhere you both are. "You sure?" she questions.

You nod. "I'm good."

Finally, the sentient vegetable shrugs and continues onward, puttering away and gradually disappearing into the distance.

As you walk onward, you're treated to an absolutely majestic sunrise, the orange glowing orb making its ascent with utter grace and bathing your journey in warm light. Your shadow stretches long across the fields, and you enjoy watching it gradually shorten as you continue along.

Fortunately, not only does your shadow change, but so does the scenery around it. It's not long before the open plains give way to the slightest bit of civilization, a few trees and forest here and there, a house or two set back off the road a ways.

Nothing seems particularly useful on your journey until, at long last, you find yourself walking past an old junkyard. The place would be fascinating regardless of your quest, all kinds of scraps piled up in strange creations, forming walls and tunnels like some kind of bizarre medieval lair.

In this particular case, however, the thing that catches your eye is the variety of different used vehicles for sale. There are a few options that've been placed around the yard, an old rusty moped to the left and a refurbished classic car on the right. Both of them feature cardboard signs sitting out before them with a surprisingly reasonable price tag.

You begin to wander deeper into the junkyard, until eventually you hear a soft rumble and catch sight of a sentient motorcycle cruising up to you. She has long dark hair and a kind smile.

"I'm Bazara," the motorcycle offers. "Something I can help you find?"

"I think so," you reply. "I'm traveling pretty far and I'm looking for a ride that won't fall apart on the way. It doesn't have to be fancy at all, just cheap and reliable."

"We can definitely find you something," the living motorcycle continues, puttering along next to you as you stroll through the stacks of junk. "Where are you headed?"

"San Diego," you reply.

Bazara glances at you awkwardly for a moment, her attitude distinctly shifting and then returning back to her usual, smiling self just moments later.

"What?" you blurt, unable to keep quiet about this unexpected mood shift.

"That's just really far!" the sentient vehicle replies with a laugh. "I think I might have something that works. Stay here and let me see if I can find it."

The living bike revs her engine and then rumbles off into the junkyard, heading deeper as she searches for the vehicle in question.

Keep looking through the vehicles on page 148
If you think something is up turn to page 174

70

You stand in silence for a moment, still reeling from what just happened, then immediately spring into action as you pull out your *SPARE TRUCK TIRE* and get to work.

It's not long before you've replaced the flat. You take a moment, wiping the sweat from your brow, then climb back up into your cab and pull out onto the road once again.

You call Truckman.

"It's late!" your boss blurts as he answers the phone. "Is everything okay?"

"No," you reply. "Definitely not okay. I just got accosted by a devil and his bigfoot henchman. They're working for Cobbler Trucking."

"Ted," your boss replies matter of factly. "Ted Cobbler."

"That's the one," you offer. "They asked me where the device was and I said I didn't know."

"And they left?" Truckman continues.

"They did," you reply. "It helps that the cargo hold was full of chocolate milk. They think they've been following the wrong truck."

Your boss breathes an audible sigh of relief, but the moment doesn't last long. "You need to get out of there," Truckman informs you. "They'll figure it out soon enough, and they'll come back angry."

"What's the device?" you demand to know, sick of all the secrets.

Truckman sighs loudly. "I suppose I can tell you now that it's come to this. What you have in your truck is something called The Big Red Button. Every timeline has one, and although they exist in a variety of different forms and shapes, they all serve the same purpose. Anyone who pushes The Big Red Button will descend deeper into The Tingleverse, traveling downward through the layers of reality."

"I'm... not entirely sure what that means," you admit.

"That's fine," Truckman explains. "Just don't push the button, and don't let if fall into the wrong hands."

"Why not push the button?" you question. "What if the next timeline is better?"

"It *is* slightly better, but that's exactly why you can't leave this one. You're here to protect the button at all costs, and if you leave this timeline there will be nobody here to look after it," your boss explains. If a scoundrel finds The Big Red Button they could easily reverse engineer it and create a device that brings *negative* timelines into this one, making the universe progressively more terrible. They could even program the button to tear this reality apart."

"I've got this," you reply confidently. "You can count on me to get The Big Red Button where it needs to go."

"I know, that's why I selected you for this trip," Truckman explains. "Now that you know what's back there, you should keep The Big Red Button on you at all times. Take it out of the cargo hold and put it in your backpack or bag."

"I would if I could," you counter. "I don't know how to get into the secret compartment."

"Just go into the back and knock on the floor of the container three times. Once that's finished, say the words 'love is real.'"

"Got it," you reply.

You drive a while longer and then finally pull off at a motel in the middle of nowhere, the first place you spot with a flickering vacancy sign. You climb into the back of your truck and follow Truckman's instructions, announcing the words "love is real" and then rapping three times on the floor with the heel of your shoe.

Immediately, a small sliding door opens up to reveal the mechanical device hidden just beneath your refrigerated chamber. It's rectangular and covered in wires, featuring an enormous red circle on one side of the box. You pull it out and carefully place it into your bag.

Wasting no time, you quickly check in and retire to your room for the evening, The Big Red Button sitting safe and sound by your side.

Awaken on page 39

72

You don't get far down the road before your curiosity gets the best of you, the specter of this secret compartment finally reaching its boiling point and spilling over within your psyche.

You pull the truck over, rumbling onto the side of the highway and shutting off the engine. You climb out of the cab and walk around to the back of your vehicle with confidence and purpose, then throw open the door with a loud rattle.

Gazing into the empty container, it's hard to believe that anything unusual is going on here. After all, there's not very much to look at. The entire vessel has been cleared out, leaving behind nothing but a rectangular box with perfectly flat sides.

You climb up into the back of your truck, taking note that this refrigerated container is just about the same temperature inside as it is outside.

Not knowing what else to do, you run your hands across the walls, making your way to every corner and knocking quietly to see if anything hollow reveals itself. No luck. Next, you try this same technique on the floor below, rapping the heel of your shoe against the hard surface.

There's a slight change in tone, but no trap door to be found. Eventually, you're forced to give up.

Maybe you're better off not finding this secret compartment anyway.

Continue into Utah on page 76

"I've got a delivery to make," you state bluntly. "I'm not letting anyone into the back of that truck."

You can tell by the looks on the faces of these creatures that this kind of refusal is not something they're used to. They're both surprised and slightly amused at the gall on display.

The lead jackalope takes one final step toward you, rearing up on his hind legs so that the already enormous rabbit can look you dead in the eyes.

"We're not violent by nature," the creature explains, "but we do what we have to do. The cold months out here can be ruthless, and a pack needs food to eat and milk to drink."

"I can't let you in there," you repeat, trembling now.

"These horns are sharp," the creature continues. "Don't make us use them."

With every passing second it's becoming clearer and clearer just how limited your options are. If you don't let them into your cargo hold, you'll end up fighting the whole pack.

Glancing around the group of vicious jackalopes, you're not quite sure if you can take them.

Fight the jackalopes on page 94
Open the truck on page 34

You take a moment to size up the figure, considering all the evidence before you and then finally making your call.

"That's just a hockey player," you announce.

The sentient potato frowns and shakes her head. "Incorrect. If that was a hockey player, he'd be wet from the ice and that water dripping off him would be cold. The water is lukewarm, so he's definitely a slashman."

The large, masked figure is almost out the door at this point, pushing through and causing the bell to jingle as he makes his exit. With a split second to spare, the potato calls out from behind, stopping him in his tracks.

"Hey!" the sentient vegetable yells, "would you mind settling a bet for us?"

The masked dinosaur slowly turns around, his vacant eyes staring into us as he continues to drip onto the tile floor below. "Sure" he finally offers, the single word falling out of his throat with a deep thud.

"Are you a hockey player or a slashman?" the potato questions.

The massive figure hesitates for a moment, breathing heavy against his mask as we wait intently for his response.

"I'm a slashman," the dinosaur finally reveals, "but it's my day off. Have a good one."

With that, the figure turns around and heads out the door, trudging onward and disappearing from sight.

You glance back at the sentient potato to see that she's shrugging with disappointment. "Sorry about that," she says. "You lost, and rules are rules. I can't give you a prize, but I *can* offer you a little piece of advice."

"Oh yeah?" you question, raising an eyebrow.

The potato nods, then gazes out through the window behind you, observing your vehicle. "Based on the make and model of your rig, and the fact that you're working for Truckman Trucking, I'd say you've got a whole lot of chocolate milk in there," she begins.

You nod, still consistently impressed by this sentient veggie.

"That's what I thought," the potato continues confidently. "The thing is, your load is balanced too heavy at the center of the cargo hold. You're putting pressure on all the wrong places. Someone loaded it up incorrectly."

You narrow your eyes in confusion, trying to see what the living potato sees but unable to make these mighty informational leaps. Still, she's proven herself thus far.

"I mean, it was the same team that always loads me up," you explain. "I don't see how they could've made a mistake."

"Well, they did," continues the potato. "I'm not saying you're gonna crash if you keep driving like that, but it's certainly not safe. You could easily crack an axel."

You consider these words, growing more and more concerned by the second.

"You want me to climb back there any take a look?" the living vegetable questions. "I could sort things out pretty quick for you, then you wouldn't have to worry about it when you're driving through the pass."

You're on a tight schedule, but if this is as dangerous as it sounds, it might be worth heeding the potato's advice.

If you trust your own loaders turn to page 87
Let the potato check things out on page 19

76

After the drama earlier in your day, it's nice to settle in and just drive. You feel comfortable here behind the wheel, and as the sun creeps its way across the sky you get a chance to finally meditate on the fact that this is your final ride.

It's been a long road to travel, both literally and otherwise, but you're happy to look back on your journey and state proudly that you did things right. You always made the delivery on time.

The gorgeous landscape gradually begins to shift and change as you cross the state line into Utah. Here, you find yourself greeted by wide open fields of seed grass that stretch on and on as far as the eye can see. In every direction, the beautiful plains seem to wave happily as you pass them by, seeing you off.

As the sun dips just below the horizon line and the sky blooms a deep purple, you find yourself bathed in a sensation of peace and tranquility.

Suddenly, however, that all changes. You glance in your rearview mirror to catch another set of headlights approaching, and approaching fast. You're not going slow by any means, which implies this visitor is coming up behind you at well over the speed limit.

Soon enough, they're pulling up in the lane right next to you. In the dying light of the day you get a full view of the enormous, black and red semi-truck, the vehicle emblazoned on the side with a familiar logo.

"Cobbler Trucking," you read aloud under your breath, immediately recognizing a member of your main competitor's fleet.

If it was up to you, you'd welcome another trucking line, and often times this is the case. There's a trucker code out here on the road, and you're always willing to help out a fellow driver in need, even if they're driving for someone else.

However, Cobbler Trucking is a different situation entirely. Everyone knows them for their bad attitude and occasional dastardly deed, a crew of hateful pirates on the highways of America.

Suddenly, the truck blasts its horn. The sound is so loud and abrupt that you jump in your seat and jerk the wheel, your heart skipping a beat as you struggle to collect yourself and keep from running off the road.

Seconds later, the rival truck takes off ahead, slamming on the gas and erupting onward at a reckless speed. You watch as they disappear into the distance, vanishing into the night.

You take a deep breath and let it out, still feeling incredibly on edge. Earlier in the drive you did a good job of blocking out the trauma of that jackalope encounter, but in this moment of weakness your anxiety comes flooding back.

"Oh shit, oh shit," you start repeating under your breath, unable to stop the words from spilling out of your mouth.

You've still got plenty of ground to cover if you want to make this delivery, but part of you is begging for a break. Maybe the safest option is to pull over and gather your thoughts for a minute.

You notice a small turn out up ahead, a perfect spot to rest should you need it.

Pull over on page 47
Keep driving on page 62

You're not exactly thrilled about this arrangement, but at the moment it sounds like the best option you've got.

"Alright, you can have my spare," you accept.

"You've got a deal!" the stegosaurus replies warmly, slapping his clawed hand on the counter with excitement then spinning around to approach the ancient hunting rifle he's got hanging on the wall nearby.

"Oh," you blurt, "is the rifle really necessary?"

The dinosaur pulls his weapon down, checking it out for a moment and then hoisting it over his shoulder by the leather strap. "You can never be too careful with jackalopes around," the dinosaur explains.

You're still not exactly comfortable with him carrying a weapon around, but your anxiety is soothed a bit by the fact that it looks like it hasn't been fired in over a hundred years.

The two of you leave the gas station and begin to head back down the hill, taking even more time than before as you avoid the larger patches of ice. It feels as though the temperature has dropped a whole ten degrees since the last time you were out here.

You're still a few yards away from the truck when suddenly your dinosaur friend raises his hand to stop you. He's listening intently for something, which causes you to follow suit.

Suddenly, your eyes go wide. It sounds like someone is attempting to break the lock off the back of your truck.

"Jackalopes," the stegosaurus says under his breath.

Before you have a chance to react he's off and running. You follow behind, and soon enough you're rounding the corner of a snow drift to discover that the dinosaur is, in fact, correct.

While you've never seen a jackalope yourself, you've heard plenty of stories about these strange creatures. They're much larger than you expected, featuring the body of an enormous hare that's topped by a set of glorious, pointy antlers.

The jackalopes have gathered around the back of your cargo hold, slamming the lock with their horns. It appears as though they've finally smashed it open, but they haven't yet had a chance to get into your chocolate milk stash.

There's an powerful bang as the dinosaur next to you points his hunting rifle into the air and fires off a thunderous warning shot. Immediately, the jackalopes scatter, the band of creatures bounding off in every direction with their frantic, hopping strides.

"Get outta here!" the stegosaurus cries.

You watch as one of the giant, rabbit-like creatures leaps right past you, making his way back up the road. He doesn't get far, however, before a fellow big-rig truck comes barreling around to corner and slams into the creature.

"Oh my god!" you blurt.

The truck doesn't even slow down, just continuing to rumble onward down the road and out of sight. The jackalope is dead.

Soon enough, the snowy scene is plunged back into a deafening silence, faint snowflakes dancing down from the sky above and landing gracefully across this glorious wilderness landscape.

You watch as the stegosaurus slowly approaches the body of what was once a jackalope.

"Is it?" you begin, already knowing the answer.

The dinosaur next to you doesn't respond. Instead, he pulls out a hunting knife and crouches next to the creature's body. You can see him working on something, sawing away with feverish intensity, but his back is blocking your view.

Moments later, he pulls something else out of his pocket, putting it all together before standing up again. The dinosaur turns around and extends a gift.

"Lucky jackalope's foot," he explains.

"Oh!" you blurt, taking the strange creation in your hands. The charm is simple enough, just a small tuft of fur with a metal cap on the end. Based on this size of this item, and the enormity of the jackalope, it's more like a lucky jackalope's *toe* than the whole foot, but it probably works just as well.

"Thanks," is all that you can think to say, putting the LUCKY JACKALOPE'S FOOT into your pocket.

The stegosaurus nods, then immediately gets to work on his next task. He strolls over to your truck and pops the hood, then begins to rummage around on the inside. He's got a small selection of tools with him and they seem to get the job done.

Moments later, the dinosaur climbs down and wipes his hands confidently. "That should do it," he offers.

"All fixed?" you reply with excitement.

80

"All fixed," the dinosaur confirms, then strolls over to your truck's cab and opens it up. He climbs inside and searches for a brief moment, then suddenly reemerges with a spare tire in his hand. "A deals a deal," the stegosaurus states bluntly.

"A deals a deal," you repeat back.

The dinosaur nods and then waves goodbye. You watch as he carries away your *SPARE TRUCK TIRE*, carefully ascending the hill and eventually disappearing from view.

It suddenly hits you just how much time has been wasted on this little detour. You've gotta get moving.

You climb back up into the driver's seat and start your engine, smiling wide as it roars to life with a familiar purr.

While other vehicles might be completely trapped in this situation, your truck is built for power. It takes a minute, but eventually you manage to back yourself out of the ditch and return to the asphalt.

Soon enough, you're off and running once again, making your way down the winding road ahead.

Continue into Utah on page 97

After giving it some thought, you finally decide to pull over on the side of the road and allow yourself a minute to rest. There's a great sense of relief as your tires crunch onto the gravel, and the second you put your rig in park and turn the keys, you realize what a good idea this little break really was.

You close your eyes, allowing the relaxation to flow through you like a cool and gentle river. It's hard to tell how long you stay like this, but by the time you open your eyes again the sun has disappeared completely, revealing a glorious, star-filled sky above.

You see now that your headlights are shining directly at a small wooden sign, a marker so inconspicuous you would've never even noticed it without stopping.

"Home of Truth, Utah," you read aloud. "Population zero."

The sign is especially curious since there are no structures to be found in the immediate vicinity, abandoned or otherwise. You do, however, notice a faint, ghostly light off in the distance. It's hard to tell exactly what it is, but it appears to be emanating from somewhere in the middle of this grassy field.

You're curious, but also a little frightened.

Investigate the light on page 132
Keep driving on page 120

82

You succumb to your gut instinct and veer to the left, sprinting in and around an assortment of busted washing machines and old, worn out refrigerators.

It quickly becomes clear that this direction is only leading you deeper into the junkyard, but before you get a chance to turn around you hear a blood curdling shriek from above you, the eagle's shadow momentarily rushing past.

Immediately, you duck down behind a pile of metal, haphazardly finding yourself right next to a rusted out oil drum. Thinking fast, you tilt up the edge and climb underneath, sealing yourself in.

You hold your breath, staying perfectly still as you peer out at this section of the scrapyard through a small hold in the barrel. The eagle flaps down and lands, this massive bird now looking even more terrifying and ferocious than it did while locked up in the cage. It struts around a bit, investigating the area while you struggle to stay perfectly motionless.

If you have the bubblegum turn to page 187
If you don't have the bubblegum turn to page 119

You remember the lucky token in your pocket and pull it out, gripping it tight as you continue to run and desperately hoping that your prayers will be answered.

Less than ten seconds later, a packed car full of dinosaurs pulls up next to you, keeping pace as the driver leans over and yells out through the window.

"You need some help?" the raptor calls.

"Yes!" you cry in return, nodding frantically.

The family of four prehistoric creatures all exchange knowing glances. The next thing you know, they're swerving in front of you and popping open the back of their hatchback. You can see that the vehicle has been stuffed full of road trip luggage, but there's still room for one more passenger to squeeze into the very back.

"Get in!" the dinosaurs cry.

You glance over your shoulder at the unicorn security guards who are right on your heels, then push yourself to make a final eruption of speed, catching up with the car and diving inside.

The dinosaurs cheer as the driver slams down onto his gas pedal, pulling out onto the road once again and leaving the unicorns behind.

"Thank you," you gush.

"No, thank you!" the driver replies, glancing back over his shoulder with a wide smile.

"He is saved!" the other raptors cheer excitedly.

Once you manage to collect yourself you sit up and greet the passengers. There is a mother and father dinosaur in front, and a son and daughter in the back. The dinosaurs are conservatively dressed, definitely not the Sin City type, and grinning so wide that it might be a little alarming if not for the fact that they've already been so kind and welcoming.

"Welcome to the Davis family road trip! I'm David Davis, this is my wife Danielle Davis and our son and daughter, Derek and Daisy Davis. Where are you headed, weary soul?" the raptor behind the wheel questions.

"San Diego," you reply.

The dinosaur exchange thrilled glances once more, utterly blown away by this discovery.

"Hallelujah!" David Davis exclaims. "It's a miracle!"

"What is?" you question, a little confused.

"Every year, the Davis family road trip starts in Salt Lake City," Mr.

Davis begins, smiling from ear to ear. "Would you like to know where it ends up?"

"Where?" you question.

The whole car exchanges yet another glance, then happily announces the answer in unison. "San Diego!"

They all cheer.

"We'd love to give you a ride!" David Davis continues.

"That's very kind. Thank you," you reply, way too exhausted to decline even if you wanted to. You sit back against the luggage, appreciating the soft bags under your weary body.

The family of raptors begin to sing along with their tape player as you settle in for a long journey.

Family road trip to page 184

There's something about this stegosaurus that you just don't trust, so you decide to continue on your way without heeding his warnings.

"I think I'll be fine," you offer confidently.

"You sure?" the dinosaur presses. "Would hate to see something bad happen out there in the snow."

His comment seems sincere, but there's something about it that puts you on edge.

"Well, I know where to hike back to if I run into any problems," you offer with a laugh.

The dinosaur doesn't react like you'd expect, not even faking a chuckle as he continues to stare. Eventually, he just nods, then turns around and heads back into his shop.

Feeling like you've made the right decision, you climb back up into your cab and put the truck in drive, heading off down the road.

Whether or not someone actually *was* tampering with the truck, you should still drive with an err of caution out here with the ice. These roads are windy and narrow, which would already be dangerous in an average sedan, but maneuvering your top-heavy truck through all this chaos is even more frightening.

Your eyes are laser focused on the road ahead as you approach a slight decline, but as you tap the breaks to curb your speed, you find yourself just continuing to accelerate.

"What the fuck!" you blurt out loud, hammering your foot down onto the brakes and realizing they've been cut.

Your mind immediately shifts into a new operating mode, accepting how dangerous this situation is and doing everything you possibly can to get yourself out of it. There's no way of slowing the truck down by traditional means, but it's still not going as fast as it soon will be.

Springing into action, you realize that you've only got one choice.

You brace yourself for impact, then turn gradually into one of the nearby snow banks, aiming for a spot where plenty of the white fluffy powder has built up.

There's a terrible rumble as you drive down into a ditch and then a loud crunch as you slam hard into the snow, your body thrown violently against your seatbelt.

Moments later, everything is silent.

You sit up, overwhelmingly sore but still in one piece. You take

86

about thirty seconds to collect yourself, then open the driver's side door and climb out into the deep snow.

Time to assess the damage.

As you trudge through the powder, you discover this situation isn't quite as dire as it could've been. You've somehow managed to hit this snow drift at just the right angle, only cosmetically damaging the front of your truck but otherwise okay. The cargo container seems perfectly fine, and although you haven't checked inside, you know these crates are packed to withstand much more chaos.

The situation is dire, but your last ride isn't a total loss just yet. You've still got plenty of time to get to San Diego, so long as you can get your brakes repaired in a reasonable amount of time.

You take a deep breath and let it out, glancing back over your shoulder in the direction you came from. Part of you wants to hike up there and call on the stegosaurus for help. He might've seemed a bit strange, but it turns out he was telling the truth. Someone actually *was* tampering with your vehicle.

On the other hand, you're pretty good at truck repair yourself. You've got some tools in the cab, so maybe you can get to the bottom of this without asking for help.

Hike back to the gas station for help on page 130
Fix it yourself on page 150

Safety is important, but your inspectors back at the warehouse are professionals who know exactly what they're doing. Besides, you've only got so much time to get down to San Diego, and you shouldn't be making a full safety check every time someone gets a hunch that the truck is loaded incorrectly.

"I think I'm gonna take my chances," you finally tell the potato, trying your best to be polite as you deny her suggestion. "Thank you so much, though."

"Your call," the living veggie replies, offering nothing more than a shrug. "Have a good trip!"

With that, you head back out to your big-rig and climb into the driver's seat. You've got a lot of road to cover, and you're trilled for whatever lies ahead.

You put the vehicle into drive and then pull away from the travel stop, headed for Utah.

Cruise into Utah on page 97

Finally, you make your choice, handing over The Big Red Button to Borson Reems.

"Thank you," the man replies warmly, softening up a bit.

This expression of warmth doesn't last long, however. Soon enough, Borson begins to laugh, a hearty chuckle bubbling up from deep within him and spilling out of his throat in and uncontrollable fit. He's cackling now, and as his vocalizations change so does his face.

The man standing before you is no longer Borson Reems, but the devilish Ted Cobbler himself.

You attempt to lunge at the bright red devil but before you can, an enormous bigfoot emerges from the shadows behind you, wrapping his enormous hairy arms around your body and holding you tight.

"Let go!" you cry out.

"You've been a thorn in our side for far too long," Ted announces gleefully.

The strength of the bigfoot is far too much to fight back against, and soon enough you find yourself bound by a heavy rope. The one-eyed bigfoot is exceptionally skilled at tying knots, rendering you completely helpless and then hoisting you up over his shoulder.

"No wait!" you cry out, but the sasquatch is on a mission now, completely ignoring your pleas.

Ted waves goodbye as you're carried out of the warehouse, the one-eyed bigfoot lumbering down a long wooden dock that extends out into the bay. In any other part of the city someone might be able to hear your cries, but in this abandoned industrial sector, there's not a soul in sight.

As you reach the end of the dock you make your final case, begging the bigfoot to let you go. "Don't do this!" you cry out. "You may be a scoundrel, but you're not a devil."

"That's what you think," the one-eyed bigfoot replies coldly, then lifts you up to hurl you off the end of the pier.

Suddenly, an enormous silver oval shimmers into existence before you, hovering over the water just a few yards out. The bigfoot stops abruptly, staring in awe at the spaceship and then erupting in a splatter of flame and guts as the vessel blasts him with its laser cannon.

You drop immediately, slamming hard against the wooden deck of the pier as the wind is knocked out of you.

Moments later, a whole squad of dinosaur space rangers teleport onto the dock in their silver suits, led by Captain Orion.

"I lied," he admits, leaning down to untie your tightly wrapped bindings. "We only pretended to leave so as to avoid any battles that might draw unwanted attention. Looks like that option is no longer on the table, so we might as well get the job done right."

Once you're freed you stand up and dust yourself off. Orion hands you a blaster, the weapon shimmering with brilliant red energy, then motions his troops toward the warehouse.

You join the group as you fan out across the side of the building, identifying every entrance and then waiting for Orion's signal. Moments later, the whole squadron of space dinosaurs are kicking in the doors and rushing inside, searching for any sign of Ted.

The devil is standing right there in the middle of the room, utterly confused but immediately springing into action. He raises his hands, a swirling green mist forming at the end of his fingertips. Before Ted gets a chance to fire off his spell, however, he's struck by a laser bolt, erupting into a million pieces and splattering everywhere.

The room falls into a powerful silence, everyone reeling from the unexpected fact that this mission is suddenly over.

The peace is shattered with a loud clatter, causing you to jump in alarm. You turn around to find the real Borson Reems, tied to a chair and laying on his side after falling out of a closet.

You rush over and free the scientist, helping him to his feet.

"I have something for you," you offer, walking over to Ted's nearby desk and picking up The Big Red Button.

You hand the device over, officially sealing your final delivery.

"Thank you," Borson gushes. "This is going to change the world. This proves love is real."

The dinosaur space troops begin to chat amongst themselves, satisfied with a job well done.

"You did great," Orion offers, strolling over to you and placing a scaly claw on your shoulder.

You're about to reply when the whole gang of prehistoric creatures suddenly disappears, teleporting away.

You stare out across the San Diego shoreline from the deck of your oceanside hotel, enjoying the beach and the glorious sunset beyond. It's your first night of retirement, and you couldn't be happier. You were hoping for an exciting last ride, after all, and that one certainly fit the bill.

You reach over and grab the glass of ice cold chocolate milk sitting next to you, taking a long, satisfying pull from the sweet and delicious beverage.

This is what it's all about.

As the sound of the ocean hums peacefully in your ears, you kick up your feet and pull out your phone, hoping to read a little bit of the local news.

You smile when you see the first headline, reading it aloud to yourself. "Witnesses report flying saucer over the water, authorities baffled."

If they only knew.

THE END

You reach into your pocket and pull out the devil's truck keys, jingling them mischievous in the air. "Looks like we're in luck," you offer.

You slip out of your car and creep along the side of the warehouse, cautiously glancing around for any sign of danger as you approach the red and black big-rig. When you reach the truck, you climb up and open the cab in complete silence, slowly sliding your pilfered keys into the ignition and then turning them ever so slightly to power on the vehicle, yet refrain from starting the engine.

You hurry back over to Riley, then crouch down next to her.

"Ready," you offer.

The sportscar begins to focus intently on Ted's truck. "I'm connecting wirelessly," she explains, then smiles when she discovers some kind of important internal connection. "Ah, there it is."

Suddenly, Ted's big-rig roars to life at a deafening volume, startling you from all the way over here. The truck begins to rumble forward, rolling down the wharf at an ever increasing speed as it hurtles toward the nearby pier.

Almost immediately, Ted and his one-eyed bigfoot companion burst out of the warehouse, sprinting after their runaway truck and leaving their prisoner completely unattended.

Now is your chance. Without a second thought you slip into the warehouse, searching through the vast industrial building until you find the closet that Riley had discovered on her scan. You open the door to reveal the real Borson Reems strapped to a chair with a gag in his mouth.

"Let's get you out of here," you blurt, quickly untying his rope and helping him to his feet.

Soon enough, you and the scientist are sprinting out toward Riley, making your escape. You erupt from the warehouse just in time to watch as Ted's truck reaches the end of the pier and hurtles over the end, blasting through the guard rail and slamming down into the water below with a glorious splash.

Ted and the one-eyed bigfoot are beside themselves with panic and anger, screaming out obesities at the end of the dock as they struggle to figure out how this happened. In a panic, one-eyed bigfoot even jumps down into the water below, as though this could somehow help the situation and bring back their precious truck.

"Let's roll," you suggest to Borson Reems as you climb into your billion dollar sportscar, closing the gull-wing doors and revving the engine.

You make a squealing U-turn and head back up the street with a wide grin on your face, unable to hide to overwhelming satisfaction you feel from this karmic turn of events.

You reach into your bag, which sits on the backseat, the pull forth The Big Red Button, handing it over to Borson.

"Here's your package," you offer, closing the book on your final delivery.

You drive off as the sun continues to rise on a brand new day, excited for whatever comes next.

THE END

Eventually, the chaos of the morning settles and fades away behind you, gradually disappearing like the mile markers in your rearview mirror. You'd expected this journey to be a relaxing last hurrah, a simple mission with little drama and plenty of road to cover, but it clearly hasn't worked out that way.

Finally, however, you get a moment to settle in. The glorious landscape of Utah stretches out in every direction as you make your crossing, beautiful mountain passes and deep valleys coming and going as the radio plays all your favorite songs.

You take a very brief dip into Arizona before finally crossing over into Nevada, the ground beneath you flattening out as it transforms into a vast, yellow desert.

By now, the sun has crept all the way across the sky and started its descent on the other side of the world, first bathing the sand and asphalt in long shadows and then causing the sky to erupt with a blossom of orange and purple.

This is what it's all about.

As this breathtaking display begins fading to black, you crest a hill and bear witness to the emerging lights of Las Vegas below. They twinkle like stars before you, coaxing you onward with the promise of fun and excitement.

Of course, fun and excitement is that last thing on your mind right now. You're utterly exhausted, having trouble keeping your eyes open as you barrel onward through the desert. For the sake of safety, it's probably a good idea to take a rest here in Las Vegas, but you're also worried that you might get a little distracted.

Stop in Las Veags on page 140
Keep driving a little longer on page 58

While the jackalopes are tough, you're tougher. They might have the advantage with these sharpened antlers, but those will only be a problem if the creatures manage to catch you. With enough bobbing and weaving, you might be able to take on the whole gang.

If that's what it takes to protect this delivery, then so be it.

In one quick movement you throw a mighty swing at the lead jackalope, trying your best to take the creature off guard and strike him directly in the face.

Unfortunately, the jackalope's reflexes are unlike anything you could've expected. The creature pulls back at twice the speed of your punch, retracting his head just enough so that your powerful swing sails past him and pulls you along with it.

You stumble forward a bit, which is all the creature needs to hunch down and then lunge upward toward your chest, goring you with his collection of sharpened spikes.

The antlers sink deep into your body, stopping you in your tracks and flooding you with a sense of overwhelming pain. You try to speak, but find nothing more than warm liquid gurgling up in your mouth and spilling down your chin.

The rest of the creatures actually gasp, previously threatening to show their power but clearly not quite ready for the consequences.

The lead jackalope pulls back a bit, extracting his horns from within as you cough and sputter. You try your best to take a deep breath, but the air refuses to come.

As the world darkens, you stagger back, reaching around for something to balance against and finding nothing but the snow drift. It crumbles under your touch. You collapse into the cold powder, unable to lift yourself back up as the white snow slowly turns to red around you.

As the light fades you feel yourself getting surprisingly warm, drifting off into the embrace of an endless darkness.

THE END

After considering your decision for a moment you finally decide on the BUBBLEGUM, which the potato plucks from its box and hands over to you.

You tear open the end and pop a slice of the delicious pink treat into your mouth, smiling with a deep satisfaction as you begin to chomp it between your teeth. There are plenty more sticks to enjoy later, should the desire arise.

"Thank you," you offer the sentient vegetable, slipping the pack of gum into your pocket.

You turn to leave but the potato suddenly calls out to stop you. When you turn back around you see that she's gazing out at your truck, her many eyes narrowed as she takes it all in.

"One last thing before you go," the living veggie offers.

"What's that?" you question, raising an eyebrow.

The potato continues gazing out through the window behind you, intently observing your vehicle. "Based on the make and model of your rig, and the fact that you're working for Truckman Trucking, I'd say you've got a whole lot of chocolate milk in there," she begins.

You nod, still consistently impressed by this sentient veggie.

"That's what I thought," the potato replies confidently. "The thing is, your load is too heavy in the center of the cargo hold. You're putting pressure on all the wrong places. Someone packed it up all wrong."

You narrow your eyes in confusion, trying to see what the living potato sees but unable to make these informational leaps. Still, she's proven herself thus far.

"I mean, it was the same team that always loads me up," you explain. "I don't see how they could've made a mistake."

"Well, they did," continues the potato. "I'm not saying you're gonna crash if you keep driving like that, but it's certainly not safe. You could easily crack an axel."

You consider these words, growing more and more concerned by the second.

"You want me to climb back there any take a look?" the living vegetable questions. "I could sort things out pretty quick for you, then you wouldn't have to worry about it while you're driving through the pass."

96

You're on a tight schedule, but if this situation is as dangerous as it sounds, it might be worth heeding the potato's advice.

If you trust your loaders and want to get moving, turn to page 87
Let the potato check things out on page 19

After the drama earlier in your day, it's nice to settle in and just drive. You feel comfortable here behind the wheel, and as the sun creeps its way across the sky you get a chance to finally meditate on the fact that this is your final ride.

It's been a long road to travel, both literally and otherwise, but you're happy to look back on your journey and say that you did things right. You always made the delivery.

The gorgeous landscape gradually begins to shift and change as you cross the state line into Utah. Here, you find yourself greeted by wide open fields of seed grass that stretch on and on as far as the eye can see. In every direction, the beautiful plains seem to wave happily as you pass them by, seeing you off.

As the sun dips just below the horizon line and the sky blooms with deep purple, you find yourself bathed in a sensation of peace and tranquility.

Suddenly, however, that all changes. You glance in your rearview mirror to catch another set of headlights approaching, and approaching fast. You're not going slow by any means, which implies this visitor is coming up behind you at well over the speed limit.

Soon enough, they're pulling up in the lane right next to you. In the dying light of the day you get a full view of the enormous, black and red semi-truck, the vehicle emblazoned on the side with a familiar logo.

"Cobbler Trucking," you read aloud under your breath, immediately recognizing a member of your main competitor's fleet.

If it was up to you, you'd welcome another trucking line, and often times this is the case. There's a trucker code out here on the road, and you're always willing to help out a fellow driver in need, even if they're driving for someone else.

However, Cobbler Trucking is another situation entirely. Everyone knows them for their bad attitude and occasional dastardly deed, a crew of hateful pirates on the highways of America.

Suddenly, the truck blasts its horn. The sound is so loud and abrupt that you jump in your seat and jerk the wheel, your heart skipping a beat as you struggle to collect yourself and keep from running off the road.

Seconds later, the rival big-rig takes off ahead of you, stepping on the gas and erupting onward at a reckless speed. You watch as they disappear in the distance ahead, vanishing into the night.

98

You take a deep breath and let it out, still feeling incredibly on edge. Your hands are trembling slightly and you're having trouble focusing.

You've still got plenty of ground to cover if you want to make this delivery, but part of you is begging for a break. Maybe the safest option is to pull over and gather your thoughts for a minute.

You notice a small turn out up ahead, a perfect spot to rest should you need it.

Pull over on page 44
Keep driving on page 4

The offer to stick around is nice enough, but you can't help shake the feeling that this little detour has already consumed too much of your time. You've got an important mission to take care of, and as exciting as this all is, you really should get going.

Besides, dancing with a ghost seems like it could have unintended consequences for the living. That's not exactly a theory you want to test right now.

"Thanks, but I really should be going," you insist, stepping back from the phantom woman.

She's a little disappointed, but manages a smile and a shrug. "I knew you we're gonna say that," she replies, then floats back to the rest of her group. They greet her warmly as they fall into another rousing dance routine.

You turn and begin the trek back to your truck, returning the way you came through this wide open field of darkness. You walk for quite a while until, suddenly, you notice something peculiar on the road ahead.

Your truck is right where you left it, but another vehicle sits parked nearby with its headlights blaring. It's the truck from Cobbler Trucking.

You duck down into the tall grass as two figures slowly walk out into their own headlights, talking amongst themselves as the they formulate a plan.

You can't make out their words from all the way over here, but you *do* manage to get a good look at the frightening characters. The first is a tall and rather imposing bigfoot, clad in a dark leather jacket and sporting an enormous beard that hangs down the front of his hairy, muscular body. He's sporting a patch over one eye.

The second backlit character to emerge from the darkness is a bright red devil, a humanoid figure with stark black hair and two long, curved horns. He has a slender tail with a point at the end, which lashes around his legs as he walks. The devil is wearing a short sleeved button up shirt, and over the heart is a name tag patch that you can just barely make out. It simply reads 'Ted.'

After a bit of discussion the bigfoot strolls around to the back of your truck. He picks up a large rock from the side of the road and smashes open the lock, then rolls up the door of your refrigerated cargo hold with a loud rattle.

Next, the bigfoot climbs up into the back of your truck and begins to go through your shipment, tearing open the crates of delicious chocolate milk and tossing them out onto the road behind him with a series of horrific smashes and crunches. You watch with absolute disgust as the entire contents of your shipment is emptied out before you, all of that glorious chocolate milk gone to waste as it pours across the glass covered ground below.

As the anger builds, you seriously consider marching back over there and giving them a piece of your mind, but you muster up all the discipline you can manage and hold back. Something much more important is at play.

"The device isn't here," the one-eyed bigfoot eventually calls out.

"What?" Ted erupts angrily. "This is the truck! It has to be there!"

The devil now springs into action, making his way around to the back of the truck and having a look for himself. The two of them continue to search, growing more and more frustrated by the second.

As someone spying on this duo from afar, their frustration only helps your cause. Their tone is much louder now, heightened to a point that you can easily hear them.

"There must be a secret door!" Ted cries out. "There's magic brewing!"

"You know magic, though," the bigfoot retorts. "You can dispel it!"

"Not like this! Not this powerful!" Ted continues, his voice bubbling over in absolute rage. "Find the driver! They must know the way in!"

The two figures hop down from the back of your truck. "You go that way and I'll go this way," you hear the bright red devil instruct, the two of them splitting off in either direction to search the field.

Fortunately, neither one of them is wandering in your exact direction yet, and there's plenty of ground for them to cover. If you stay here long enough they'll certainly to find you, but at least you've got a moment to think.

At this point, a few courses of action come to mind.

The simplest answer is to make a run for it out here in the field, leaving your rig behind and waiting until the coast is clear to make my return. Maybe you could even trek back to the ghost's and ask for their help. Of course, the longer these two unsavory characters have your truck in their possession, the more likely they are to find the secret compartment.

One solution might be to creep over there and find the device this devil and his bigfoot companion are looking for before they ever get a chance to steal it themselves.

The bravest answer, however, is as tempting as it is dangerous. As the bigfoot and the devil get farther and farther away from their own vehicle, it crosses your mind that you could sneak over there, snatch their keys, then take off in your own truck while leaving them stranded.

The only thing for certain is that you can't wait any longer to act.

Run deeper into the field on page 32

Sneak over and search for the device yourself on page 180

Steal their keys, then take off in your truck on page 48

102

You make your choice, staying low to the ground as you sneak between your tuck and theirs. You try your best to avoid the brilliant glare of their idling headlights, taking the long way around, but you eventually end up hidden in the shadows next to Ted's big-rig.

This vehicle, courtesy of Cobbler Trucking, has been left unlocked, and you gasp excitedly as you find that the keys have been left in the ignition. You swiftly pull out the DEVIL KEYS and put them in your pocket.

The headlights immediately shut off, which has most certainly alerted Ted and his bigfoot companion.

"Hey!" the devil cries out in confusion from the darkness.

Your eyes on the prize, you hurry back over to your own vehicle and climb into the driver's seat. Once there, you waste no time starting it up with a loud roar.

As your headlights illuminate the grass before you, you see Ted with a look of absolute shock plastered across his face. He immediately points a long, clawed finger at you, attempting to cast some kind of a spell, but you're too far away at this point and his dark magic doesn't work.

You start to laugh, then honk twice as you haul off down the road, literally leaving these two criminals in the dust as you continue on your way. Watching in the rearview mirror, you see them climb into their truck and then start yelling wildly, upset to discover that their keys are missing.

You drive like mad, not satisfied with pulling over until you've put as many miles between you and the other truck as possible. Eventually, however, the pounding of your heart begins to subside.

Looking for an explanation, you decide to call Truckman.

The phone barely rings once before your boss picks up, his familiar voice sounding out through your speakers. "What's up?" he questions.

"I was about to ask you the same thing!" you blurt. "I just got attacked by a devil and a bigfoot from Cobbler Trucking. They want the device but they couldn't find it."

Truckman lets out a long sigh, as though his deepest fears are coming true. "Are you okay?" he questions.

"Yeah," you reply, "but barely."

"I'm sorry to bring you into this," Truckman offers, "but you're the only one I trust on this job. The device you're carrying is called The Big Red Button. Whoever pushes that button will be sent to another timeline that is slightly more full of love."

"Sounds nice right about now," you admit.

"It does," Truckman retorts, "but you can't push it. At least, not yet. You need to stick around in this layer of reality to make sure this device gets to San Diego. There's a scientist there who will use it to prove even more love, but if The Big Red Button falls into the wrong hands it could be reverse engineered into something terrible. It could tear apart the fabric of this very timeline."

You nod along to these words, fully understanding your mission. You have no intention of letting The Big Red Button fall into Ted's claws, especially not on your final ride.

"You can count on me, boss," you tell Truckman.

"I know," he replies. "Now that they're aware you've got the device in your truck, you should take it out of the secret compartment and keep it on you at all times. The magic lock is simple enough, just got back there and knock three times, then say 'love is real.'"

"That's it?" you retort.

"That's it," Truckman continues. "Devils have a really hard time with that last phrase."

You say your goodbyes then hang up, continuing on into the night with a newly renewed sense of purpose. You make sure to turn off the main drag a bit before finding your motel for the evening.

When you finally pull into the parking lot you're absolutely exhausted. Still, there's one thing left to do.

You exit the cab and head around to the back of your truck, then climb up into the cargo hold. It's completely empty, and the idea of some secret compartment hidden within these four flat, blank walls is hard to believe.

You take a deep breath and let it out, then knock three times on the wall of your truck with your hand. "Love is real," you state confidently.

Nothing happens.

Your brow furrowed, you try this process again, this time moving over to the other side of the refrigerated truck. You knock again and say the magic words, yet your results are the same.

Growing worried, you decide to give it one last go. This time, you rap your heel against the floor of the truck.

"Love is real," you say aloud.

104

Suddenly, there's a loud clang and a hiss as a panel slides up and over, magical energy wafting up from within this tiny hidden chamber. You bend down and carefully withdraw a small box, which is covered in wires and sporting an enormous red button on the top. You carefully place it in your bag, then climb down from the back of the truck and close it up.

Until you reach San Diego, this bag isn't leaving your sight.

Get some rest on page 39

You succumb to your gut instinct and veer to the right, sprinting in and around an assortment of busted television sets and old worn out ovens.

Fortunately, it appears that your intuition was correct. Soon enough, you're bursting out of the scrapyard and sprinting down the road as fast as you can. You glance back over your shoulder to see the eagle remains preoccupied with searching the maze, circling low as the distance grows between you and this vicious predator.

You kick things into high gear and don't let up, sprinting back to the motel as fast as your legs can carry you. When you arrive, you pull out your newly pilfered tin of MAGIC BOOT CREAM, scooping out a huge glob of the strange, shimmering substance and then wiping it all over the boot that's been attached to your front wheel.

The goop sizzles with a swirling magical energy, emitting a strange hiss as it works its magic. You watch in amazement as the powerful compounds begin to react, and moments later the automotive boot emits a loud clang as it splits open and releases your truck from its metallic grasp.

No time to waste, you throw open the door of your cab and climb in, then start up your trusty big-rig with a deafening roar. As you pull out onto the road once more, you find yourself unable to stop smiling, blown away by the adventure that your final ride has unexpectedly become.

Keep on truckin' on page 93

You decide to take the most direct and efficient round, heading through the great state of Idaho with the windows down and the music blasting. It's a great start to your trip, a freeway drive you've done more times than you can count, but never seems to get old.

The landscape is pretty great, too, and once you're in it, it's hard to believe this particular route was the slightly less scenic one.

You're pleasantly lost in your thoughts, but gradually something starts pulling you back into the present. You can't help but notice that another truck seems to be following you. It's quite a ways back, but it's consistently there just rumbling along.

Of course, this is a very common trucking route, and it's not unheard of for you to notice other vehicles tagging along for an entire cross country journey. Something about this just feels different, however. It's hard to make out the colors from this far away, but they appear to be a combination of blood red and jet black.

You continue glancing in the rear view mirror as you speed up a bit, pushing the limits and eventually pulling ahead of this mysterious truck. Soon enough, it's nothing but a distant memory behind you.

Of course, speeding up like this has more advantages than just losing a possible tail: it also gets you where you're going that much quicker. When you finally pull off the road for a new tank of gas, you're pleasantly surprised by just how deep into Idaho you've managed to travel.

You fill up at the pump and then stroll into the convenience store to check out the snacks.

"Welcome!" a large, sentient potato calls over from behind the counter. She's covered in eyes, all of which track you closely.

"Hey there," you reply, then go about your business searching for something to eat.

You make your way around the small store, eventually arriving back at the counter where the potato remains. You're having trouble deciding what to get, or even accepting that you want anything at all. Maybe you just needed a moment to stretch your legs.

"How's the trip?" the sentient potato questions, nodding out toward your truck.

"Good, good," you reply. "Didn't realize how much ground I was covering."

"Good on ya," the potato continues with an appreciative nod. "Just make sure you don't push it too hard. Stay safe out there."

"Thanks, I will," you reply.

"How's the weather up there in Billings?" the potato questions.

A confused look crosses your face. You don't ever remember telling her that's where you were coming from.

"How did you know that?" you ask, startled.

The sentient potato smiles. "When you've got this many eyes you tend to notice things," she explains. "I spotted the reddish hue from the dirt on your shoes, that's a dead giveaway. Dirt here in Idaho is a lot lighter, and anything past Billings gets a little more vibrant."

"That's really something," you reply, still a bit skeptical. You glance down at your shirt, trying to remember whether or not you wore a Billings Mustang's jersey or something. Maybe this potato is just messing with you and having a laugh.

"Don't believe me, huh?" she continues.

You shrug. "I don't know what to say."

"How about this," the potato offers. "We'll have ourselves a little contest over our powers of observation. If you win, you can pick out a small item from up here at the counter."

"What if I lose?" you ask.

The potato laughs. "Then I get to brag about it."

"Fair enough," you reply.

Suddenly, the door to the gas station chimes as an enormous, broad shouldered figure walks in. It's a dinosaur of some kind, but you're not exactly sure what species because their face is covered by a hockey mask. The figure is clad in tattered, ragged clothing and dripping wet. In one hand, they hold a large carving knife covered in what appears to be blood, but in the other hand they carry a hockey stick.

You and the potato watch as the masked dinosaur slowly walks up to a nearby standing refrigerator, opening the glass door and reaching in to pull out a cold carton of chocolate milk. They slowly turn and then march up to the counter right next to you.

The mysterious dinosaur sets down his milk without a word as the lukewarm water begins to pool around your fingers. Realizing how close you are, you suddenly step back, creating a bit of distance, but the figure doesn't even acknowledge your presence.

"That'll be two dollars," the potato informs the masked dinosaur.

The masked figure pulls out two crumpled, wet bills and drops them onto the counter, then takes his chocolate milk and slowly walks back toward the door from which he entered.

"Okay," the potato whispers to you under her breath. "Is that a hockey player or a slashman?"

Guess it's a hockey player on page 74
Guess it's a slashman on page 37

"I'm just not equipped for that," you insist. "The garage owner will be out here in just a moment, though. He's a good mechanic and I'm sure he'd love to help you."

The mysterious figure finally accepts this response and turns away, sauntering through the store and checking out the various snacks and beverages for sale. You keep your eyes trained closely on this strange, trench coat wearing entity, trying to make sense of their peculiar wobble and usual height.

Eventually, the figure makes their way over to the chocolate milk section, opening up the standing refrigerator and rummaging around a bit.

"Hey!" comes an angry voice from behind you.

You glance over your shoulder to see that the dinosaur has emerged from his auto garage, and he's not happy about this stranger being in the store. When your gaze returns to the figure in the trench coat, you see them drop a giant carton of chocolate milk onto the floor in surprise, spilling the delicious brown liquid everywhere.

Before your very eyes, the coat begins to disassemble, falling away to reveal three enormous jackalopes sitting on one another's shoulders. The creatures bound toward the door as your dinosaur friend runs after then, screaming obscenities and waving his fists.

The jackalopes hop off into the snow, disappearing from sight. There's no catching them now.

The stegosaurus takes a deep breath and shakes his head, then turns back around and strolls over to you. He drops your truck keys into your hand. "All finished," he states proudly.

You pay the dinosaur for his time, and soon enough you're climbing back into the driver's seat of your truck as it purrs warmly. As you pull away from the garage and back onto the road, you catch one final glimpse of one of the strange, antlered rabbits as it stares daggers into you from beyond the nearby snowbank.

You smile and settle in for the long drive ahead.

Continue through Utah on page 97

110

After considering your decision for a moment you finally decide on the LUCKY UNICORN SHOE keychain, which the potato plucks off its tiny hanger and hands over to you.

You turn the shiny object in your hand, admiring the craftsmanship a moment before placing it on your keys and then slipping them back into your pocket.

"Thank you," you offer the sentient vegetable.

You turn to leave but the potato suddenly calls out to stop you. When you spin back around you see that she's gazing out at your truck, her many eyes narrowed as she takes it all in.

"One last thing before you go," the living veggie offers.

"What's that?" you question, raising an eyebrow.

The potato continues gazing out through the window behind you, observing your vehicle. "Based on the make and model of your rig, and they fact that you're working for Truckman Trucking, I'd say you've got a whole lot of chocolate milk in there," she begins.

You nod, still consistently impressed by this sentient veggie.

"That's what I thought," the potato replies confidently. "The thing is, your load is too heavy in the center of the cargo hold. You're putting pressure on all the wrong places. Someone packed it up all wrong."

You narrow your eyes in confusion, trying to see what the living potato sees but unable to make these informational leaps. Still, she's proven herself thus far.

"I mean, it was the same team that always loads me up," you explain. "I don't see how they could've made a mistake."

"Well, they did," continues the potato. "I'm not saying you're gonna crash if you keep driving like that, but it's certainly not safe. You could easily crack an axel."

You consider these words, growing more and more concerned by the second.

"You want me to climb back there any take a look?" the living vegetable offers. "I could sort things out pretty quick for you, then you wouldn't have to worry about it when you're driving through the pass."

You're on a tight schedule, but if this is as dangerous as it sounds, it might be worth heeding the potato's advice.

If you trust your loaders and want to get moving, turn to page 87
Let the potato check things out on page 19

You'd love nothing more than to stop the bigfoot in his tracks, but you also recognize the dark magic at Ted's disposal is much more powerful than anything you're prepared to face head on. You've gotta be smart about this, and sometimes that means staying put and waiting for your moment to arrive.

Once every crate has been opened and bottle has been smashed, the bigfoot returns to you and the devil, shaking his head from side to side. "I can't find the device," the bigfoot informs Ted. "There's gotta be a secret compartment back there."

The devil immediately turns his attention back to you, his eyes overflowing with wrath. "Where is it?" Ted shouts, raising his hands up to give you another blast of pain waves.

"I don't know!" you blurt. "I have no idea!"

The devil stops, lifting an eyebrow curiously. He seems unexpectantly impressed by your words. "You really *don't* know how to get into the secret compartment, do you?" he questions.

"I have no idea," you state firmly.

The devil begins to laugh, but this abrupt change in mood doesn't set you at ease. He's too unpredictable to know what's coming next.

Suddenly, Ted thrusts his hands out toward you again, and this time a cascade of swirling green energy erupts from his fingertips, wrapping itself around your body and pulling tight. You cry out in surprise as your frame begins to change shape, shrinking down and pulling inward as your skin hardens into scale. The sound of your voice morphs into a long hiss, and soon enough you find yourself lying flat in the middle of the road, staring up from a new, much smaller body.

Ted has turned you into a snake.

While these reptiles are quite fast when they want to be, you're too shocked to take any immediate action. Before you get a chance to slither away, the giant bigfoot reaches down and grabs ahold of your long green body, picking you up and dropping you into a bucket.

You open your mouth to cry out, but can't find a way to form the words. Instead, you focus this energy into climbing out and escaping, but the bigfoot swiftly covers the top of your container with a sturdy piece of flat wood.

You remain trapped like this for quite a while, listening as the bigfoot and devil tear your truck apart in search of their mysterious and illusive device. Of course, they never find it.

"It's not here boss," you finally hear the bigfoot say.

"It's here," he replies. "It's hidden well, but there's a secret compartment somewhere. We'll take it to Bazara."

"The lock wizard," the bigfoot offers reverently.

There's a series of loud clangs and eventually the cacophony of your truck roaring to life, hotwired up and ready to go. It appears both vehicles are prepped for the journey ahead.

Moments later, the weight of your bucket begins to shift. You're being lifted in the air and carried somewhere, then set down roughly on what you can only assume is a truck bench.

The familiar rumble of a motor beneath your body lets you know that you're on your way.

Your journey continues on page 157

The anger bubbling up inside you is just too much.

"Get out of there!" you cry, then turn away from the devil, marching toward the back of your truck with a purpose and fury in your stride.

You only get a few steps before another powerful wave of pain erupts through your body, but this time you're ready for it. You focus all of your energy on continuing forward, pushing through the horrible sensations and maintaining your balance. Unfortunately, Ted's dark magic is just too powerful, and soon enough you're collapsing to the asphalt in a heap of searing agony.

You twist and turn on the ground, completely losing control of your body as your teeth clench tight and your muscles spasm.

"I don't like to repeat myself," the devil says menacingly as he stands over you, his hand stretched out in a gnarled claw. "So I'm not going to."

Ted twists his fingers even more, elevating the pain well past anything that you could've previously imagined. It feels as though your blood is boiling, and in the throughs of this horrific pressure you can sense your heart hammering away at a speed that is simply impossible to maintain.

Your mouth is wide open but you're well past the point of being able to scream, completely overwhelmed in the worst of ways.

When you slip away it feels like a sweet relief, the pain finally subsiding as it's replaced by an eternal darkness.

THE END

Remembering that you've got a lucky jackalope's foot in your pocket, you pull it out and give the furry nub a massage with your fingers, hoping to brush off a little of the magic for yourself.

Who knows if it will actually work.

You sit back down at the blackjack table just in time for the game to start up yet again, the cards coming out and everyone taking an excited look at what they've got. There's a slight gasp when your two cards are revealed.

"Blackjack," the dealer announces, handing you your winnings.

Surely this must be a coincidence, you think, but after the next few hands you begin to think that your lucky jackalope's foot might be working a lot harder than you initially thought.

Gradually, the other players start to bust out, dropping the field down to just you and Keith the jet plane.

"I've gotta say, and I mean this in the nicest way possible, but you're the luckiest person I've ever met," Keith informs you. "You've been on a hell of a run."

"Thanks," you reply, not knowing what else to say.

The dealer suddenly interrupts your conversation, motioning toward Keith. "Would you like to hit or stand?" he questions.

"I don't care," Keith replies.

"You need to choose, sir," the dealer continues.

The jet plane shrugs, amused. "I quit then, give my friend here the grand prize."

Your eyes go wide. "Wait, what?" you blurt.

"It's fine," Keith explains "I'm a billionaire already, so I don't care about the money, I care about the adventure. I just do The World Series Of Blackjack for fun."

Alarm bells start going off as confetti begins to fall from the ceiling above you.

"We have a winner!" the dealer announces, springing to his feet.

You stand up as a crowd of onlookers begin to clap excitedly. You'd certainly hoped to make it this far, but now that you're here it seems like some kind of bizarre dream.

You reach into your pocket and give the lucky jackalope's foot one last rub of thanks.

Suddenly, the commotion of bells and whistles around you is cut but the roar of a powerful engine. You glance over to see a beautiful chrome sportscar rolling down an isle of slot machines, it's gull-wing doors opening up and beckoning you within.

"Hey there," comes a soft, silky voice from the vehicle. "I'm Riley, the car."

"Oh, hi!" you blurt in response.

"Wanna get out of here?" she continues.

You turn around and thank Keith the billionaire jet plane for kindly dropping out.

"Don't mention it," Keith replies with a smile. "Now I just gotta find the next fresh journey. Something new and different."

"You know, being a trucker is pretty exciting," you offer. "I did it for a long time, and now that I'm on my last ride I think I'm really gonna miss it."

The sentient jet plane seems intrigued. "The open road, huh?"

You suddenly remember that you've got two vehicles to travel in now. Instead of figuring out what to do with your big-rig, maybe someone else would like to carry the torch for a while.

You reach into your pocket and pull out the keys to your truck, dropping them into Keith's hand. "Head to Billings and talk to Truckman," you offer. "He'll have a few adventures for you."

The sentient plane shakes his head in amazement, then gives you a powerful hug. He's overwhelmed with gratitude and appreciation. "Thank you so much," Keith gushes.

"Have fun," you reply, then turn around and climb into the driver's seat of your brand new sportscar.

An assortment of screens and readouts appear before you, popping up like the holographic displays in some science fiction masterpiece.

"Just so you know, there's a unit of unicorn security guards approaching from the East," Riley informs you. "They're coming to haul you in for cheating."

"Wait, what?" You blurt, utterly confused.

A display suddenly pops up of six unicorns in a dark suits and sunglasses pushing their way through the crowd of gamblers. "Judging by their elevated heart rates and the dilation of their pupils, they're preparing to lie to you," the sentient car continues. "You have not actually been caught cheating. It's a ruse."

"But why?" you question aloud.

"I'm not sure, maybe they're working for someone who has it out for you?" Riley continues. "I don't think we should stick around and find out."

A chill runs down your spine as you hear this, realizing now that Ted could be lurking somewhere nearby. "You're right, let's get out of here."

You throw the car into drive and take off through the casino, rumbling out into the hotel lobby and just barely fitting through the doors to the outside world.

You glance in the rearview mirror to see the unicorns running after you, but now that you're out on the strip you have plenty of room to pick up speed. With a loud roar from Riley's engine the two of you erupt forward, the force of your momentum pulling you back against the seat behind.

You'll be in San Diego in no time.

It's sunrise as you pull up to the wharf, the glorious blue ocean stretching out before you as golden sunlight dances across the waves. Your windows down, you can already sense to wonderful feeling of sea air against your face, and only wish there were circumstances less tense for you to enjoy it.

Before you is a large industrial warehouse constructed from cheap metal sheets and typically used to hold boats or cargo shipments as they wait for a transfer. This is the address.

You glance down at your phone, reminding yourself of the scientist that you're looking for. Truckman has sent you a photograph, and you read the name below it aloud to yourself.

"Borson Reems," you say, taking in this middle aged man's enormous white beard and round nose. He has a kindness in his expression that is truly something to behold.

Riley emits a strange, dancing collection of laser beams from her dashboard, the array sweeping across the face on your phone and scanning the image.

"There are two lifeforms within the building who match this photograph," Riley announces.

"Two?" you blurt. "What do you mean?"

118

Another holographic display suddenly appears before you, floating in the air as a three dimensional projection of the warehouse. You can clearly see a man who looks very similar to Borson Rooms standing in the middle of the room, but a projection of this same figure is also tied to a chair and gagged in a nearby closet. Lurking in the shadows is the sturdy frame of a large, hairy bigfoot.

"It's a trap," you realize.

"I also detect a rather large big-rig parked on the other side of this structure," Riley announces. "I could hack into its navigation system and provide a great distraction, but only if the truck is on. We'd need the keys."

If you have the devil keys turn to page 91
If you don't have the devil keys turn to page 51

You watch in utter terror as the eagle draws closer and closer to your hiding spot, the enormous bird searching high and low as he pecks his way around in the dirt for hidden clues. There must be something that's drawing the beast toward you, some deep and powerful instinct that makes him the elite hunter he is.

Thankfully, however, the bird seems to lose interest, hopping off in the other direction and disappearing from your line of sight.

Once the coast is clear you let out a final, soft breath, overwhelmed with gratitude, but this second this happens is the second disaster strikes. Suddenly, a huge predatory eye appears in the hole you've been staring through, angry and enormous.

You scream as the massive bald eagle slams into the barrel, tipping it over and revealing you fully. In a fraction of a second the massive bird is upon you, screeching wildly and slashing you with its daggerlike talons. You struggle to defend yourself, throwing up your arms and cowering in fear, but these feeble attempts at protection are no match for this vicious hunter.

You can feel blood running down your body as you back farther and farther away, the eagle continuing to peck and claw. Your vision blurs and then begins to fade to black as you collapse into the dirt entirely, the bird still ripping at your flesh as you float off into the darkness.

THE END

120

It takes a hearty amount of mental fortitude, but you somehow manage to pull yourself together and focus on the task at hand. Maybe it's the mission itself that keeps you in line, a singular goal to maintain while everything else swirls past; a lighthouse in the storm.

You plow ahead as the sun disappears completely, but only a few miles have passed when disaster strikes.

Without warning, your headlights reveal a tire strip laid out across the road before you, a long thin row of spikes that are specifically designed to pierce the rubber of your tires.

There's a loud, earsplitting bang and now the truck is losing control, shuddering with terrifying power as you struggle to maintain a straight path along the empty highway. You can feel the back of your rig fishtailing from side to side, and for a moment you get a sense the whole thing is going to tip right over.

Fortunately, this doesn't happen.

Soon enough, you're pulling off onto the side of the road and slowing to a stop, the flap of a ragged tire sounding loud in your ear.

You open up the door of your cab and leap down onto the gravel to assess the damage. Your truck is built to withstand a lot, and the strip only managed to puncture one of your tires. Still, that's more than enough damage to keep you from going anywhere for the time being.

Even more pressing, however, is the terrifying question that repeats itself over and over again in your head, a warning alarm at the forefront of your mind. Who laid this trap?

Without warning, a pair of headlights slice through the darkness before you. The red and black Cobbler Trucking big-rig reveals its enormous and terrifying shape, parked on the side of the road just a few yards away. The vehicle begins to slowly creep forward.

Run and hide in the field on page 124
Stay and confront them on page 146

While this figure in the long trench coat is certainly strange, you don't see any reason why you shouldn't take a moment to help them out.

"Sure," you finally agree with a nod.

You stroll around the counter and head out into the cold air once again, the stranger following right behind you.

"Where's the car?" you question, but before you receive your answer you feel a hard thump against the back of your head and a split second of pain erupting across your body.

You open your eyes slowly, struggling to gather your senses as you reach back and rub the enormous lump on of your skull. The second you touch this part of your body you wince, pulling your fingers away. Something must've hit you exceptionally hard to create a knob like that.

You sit up and find that you've been wrapped in the same long trench coat that the figure was wearing. The entity, of course, is nowhere to be found.

You glance around to see that you're sprawled out in the deep snow, laying against a powdery drift and shivering profusely. Another few minutes out here and you likely wouldn't have woken up at all.

Carefully, you climb to your feet, still reeling from the pain. From here, you can see that you're not very far from the gas station, but a gasp escapes your throat when you realize that your truck is missing.

You immediately erupt in a sprint, heading toward the gas station with a body that barely functions. The cold weather has hardened your muscles and given you a painful limp, but you do everything you can to fight your way through it as you burst back into the gas station.

"Hello?" you cry out. "Where's my truck?"

There's a rustling sound from the auto garage and seconds later the familiar stegosaurus emerges. "I was about the ask you the same thing," he replies angrily. "You took off without paying!"

"That wasn't my fault!" you protest. "I was knocked out, laying behind the hill over there."

A knowing look suddenly makes its way across the dinosaur's face. "The jackalopes," he says aloud, to himself more than anyone else.

Suddenly, it all makes sense. The figure in a trench coat was nothing more than a few of these creatures stacked on top of one another, just waiting for an opportunity to steal your truck and the cargo within.

"Oh shit," you blurt out loud. "The delivery. Can I use your phone?"

The stegosaurus nods and you rush over to the counter, picking up his phone and dialing Truckman's number.

"Who's this?" Truckman begins as he answers abruptly.

"It's me," you reply.

"Oh," your boss blurts, clearly a little confused why you're not calling him on your cell phone, which has been lost along with the big-rig. "What's going on? Is everything alright?"

"No," you reply desperately, shaking your head. "Someone stole the truck."

"What?" Truckman blurts, even more alarmed than you expected.

"All the chocolate milk is gone," you continue.

Your boss hesitates for a moment, then his tone changes completely. He's no longer upset, just strangely hollow. He sounds as though he's trapped in a battle that he knows he's already lost, accepting his fate.

"There was more than just chocolate milk in that truck," Truckman admits. "There was... a device."

"A device?" you repeat back, suddenly growing even more concerned.

"The secret to unraveling this timeline, and the next," Truckman explains. "In the hands of someone who knows how to use it, the device could bring about a new era of love and kindness. In the hands of a devil, it would be a disaster."

"What about in the hands of someone who didn't know how to use it?" you continue.

"That depends," your boss continues. "First, they'd have to find it, which is difficult but not impossible. How long has it been gone?"

"A long time," you reply.

"Then it might already be too late," Truckman informs you.

The way that your boss's last work hits your ear is a little off, distorted slightly. You pull the phone away to see that the device is breaking apart in an utterly bizarre way, stretching out and floating off into space. Soon enough, your arm is extending as well, and as you watch in horror the entire gas station begins to shift and alter.

The timeline is coming apart.

"Oh no," is all that you have time to murmur before your face disappears, scattering into a thousand pieces as the universe crumbles in on itself.

THE END

You immediately spring into action, taking off into the grass at a full sprint. Soon enough, you're enveloped in the darkness of the night, hidden away as you watch from afar.

It appears the occupants of this other vehicle are more interested in your truck than they are you, as they refuse to give chase. Instead, two figures slowly walk out into their own headlights, talking amongst themselves as the they formulate a plan.

You can't make out their words from all the way over here, but you do manage to get a good look at the frightening characters. The first is a tall and rather imposing bigfoot, clad in a dark leather jacket and sporting an enormous beard that hangs down the front of his hairy, muscular body. He also has a patch covering one eye.

The second backlit form to emerge from the darkness is a bright red devil, a humanoid figure with stark black hair and two long, curved horns. He has a slender tail with a point at the end, which lashes around his legs as he walks. The devil is wearing a short sleeved button up shirt, and over the heart is a name tag patch that you can just barely make out. It simply reads 'Ted.'

After a bit of discussion the bigfoot strolls around to the back of your truck. He picks up a large rock from the side of the road and smashes open the lock, then rolls up the door to your cargo hold with a loud rattle.

Next the bigfoot climbs up into the back of the truck and begins to go through your shipment, tearing open the crates of delicious chocolate milk and tossing them out onto the road behind him with a series of horrific smashes and crunches. You watch in absolute disgust as the entire contents of your truck is emptied out before you, all of that glorious chocolate milk gone to waste as it pours across the glass covered ground below.

As the anger within you builds, you seriously consider marching back over there and giving them a piece of your mind, but you muster up all the discipline you can manage and hold yourself back. Something much more important is at play.

"The device isn't here," the bigfoot eventually calls out.

"What?" Ted erupts angrily. "This is the truck! It has to be there!"

The devil now springs into action, making his way around to the back of the truck and having a look for himself. The two of them continue to search, growing more and more frustrated by the second.

As someone spying on them from afar, this frustration only helps your cause. Their voices are much louder now, heightened to a point that you can easily hear them.

"There must be a secret door!" Ted cries out. "There's magic brewing!"

"You know magic, though," the bigfoot retorts. "You can dispel it!"

"Not this powerful!" Ted continues, his voice bubbling over with absolute rage. "Find the driver! They must know the way in!"

The two figures hop down out of the back of their truck. "You go that way and I'll go this way," you hear the bright red devil instruct, the two of them splitting off in either direction to search the field.

Fortunately, neither one of them is wandering in your exact direction yet, and there's plenty of ground for them to cover. If you stay here long enough, they'll certainly find you, but at least you've got a moment to think.

At this point, a few courses of action come to mind.

The simplest answer is to make a run for it out here in the field, leaving your rig behind and waiting until the coast is clear to make your return. Of course, the longer these two have your Truck in their possession, the more likely they are to find the secret compartment.

One solution might be to creep over there and find the device this devil and his bigfoot companion are looking for before they ever get a chance to steal it themselves.

The bravest answer, however, is the most tempting and the most dangerous. As the bigfoot and the devil get farther and farther away from their own vehicle, it crosses your mind that you could sneak over there, snatch their keys, then take off if your own truck and leave them stranded.

The only thing for certain is that you can't wait any longer to act.

Run deeper into the fields on page 32
Search for the device yourself on page 180
Take their keys and get out of there on page 48

126

You immediately realize that, without a spare tire, there's no way you're getting out of here any time soon. By the time you find your way to a shop and then back to your truck, Ted might've already realized his mistake and returned with a vengeance.

Not knowing what else to do, you pick up the phone and call Truckman.

"What's up?" your boss answers almost immediately, as though he's been sitting by his phone just in case you needed help on your journey.

"Cobbler Trucking just showed up and ransacked the shipment," you blurt.

"The milk doesn't matter. Did they find the device?" your boss immediately demands to know.

"I'm not sure," you admit.

Truckman lets out a long sigh, recognizing that plans have changed. While it had once been useful to keep you in the dark about the true nature of your journey, it's time to finally spill the beans.

"Go into the back of the truck and knock three times on the floor, then say the words 'love is real'", Truckman instructs. "That's how you open the secret compartment."

You follow his instructions, climbing up into the back of the refrigerated cargo hold and walking out into the middle of the vast, empty space. It feels strange without any of the chocolate milk in here.

You rap your heel against the ground three times. "Love is real," you announce confidently.

There's a loud clang as a panel slides up and over, magical energy wafting from within this tiny hidden chamber. You bend down and carefully withdraw a small box, covered in wires and sporting an enormous red button on the top. You carefully place it in your bag, then climb down from the back of the truck and close it up.

"I've got the device," you inform your boss.

"What you're holding is The Big Red Button," Truckman explains. "Anyone who presses it will transport into a timeline with slightly more love, which is great, but you can't press it just yet. We need you here in *this* reality to protect The Big Red Button. You've gotta get it to San Diego before it has a chance to fall into the wrong hands. If Ted Cobbler reverse engineers that machine, he could destroy the very fabric of this timeline."

"I've got this," you reply, then glace over at the shredded tire of your truck. "I just don't have a ride."

"What?" your boss blurts.

"The truck is out of commission and I don't have a spare," you inform him.

Truckman shakes this news off quickly. "Just make the delivery, it doesn't matter how."

"Okay," you reply.

"Just don't fly!" he suddenly cries out. "The Big Red Button can't handle the pressure."

"Understood," you confirm, then hang up the phone.

With no other options available, you start walking.

As you continue on your way, your eyes begin to adjust to the darkness even more, the wide open plains opening up to you in every direction. The stars above seem even more brilliant than before, and for a while you actually get to appreciate the stillness and beauty of it all. Sure, you're on an important mission, but right now it feels like the only thing that matters is appreciating the glorious size of the universe that hangs above.

You walk all night, and the entire time not a single car comes down this road to pass you by. As the dawn breaks, however, a modest yellow sedan comes puttering along from behind. Eventually, the car pulls over next to you, the rising sun casting the driver's face with a beautiful golden glow as they roll down their window.

A sentient corn on the cob sits in the vehicle before you, her body partially wrapped in a green leafy shell while the rest features rows of yellow kernels.

"Need a ride?" the sentient corn asks.

You immediately pick up on good vibes from this living vegetable, but you also remember that you can never be too sure on a mission like this.

"Where are you headed?" you question.

"Started in Nebraska, driving down to Vegas," she explains.

That covers most of the distance between here and San Diego, you immediately realize.

Take the ride on page 161
Decline her offer on page 68

The logical part of your brain knows that you should probably stay focused on the task at hand, but there's something about this bizarre, dancing illumination that takes hold of your curiosity and simply refuses to let go.

You climb out of your cab and lock up the truck, then begin your journey out into the tall grass. Your eyes quickly begin to adjust to the night, and while you still need to maintain a careful, slow pace, you do a pretty good job of getting where you're going. Fortunately, there's not much out here in the middle of nowhere for you to trip over.

As you grow closer and closer to the light, you begin to hear the sweet sound of music floating across the plains. It's an upbeat song played on fiddle, banjo and guitar, but there's also something distinctly haunting and melancholy about it.

Soon enough, you find yourself at the edge of a small ghost town, a collection of old wooden buildings set in the dirt around a central square, and not much else. The square is populated by several figures, however, and you gasp when you see them.

It appears there's a party going on, with singing and dancing abound. The revelers are all clad in old clothing, like settlers from way back when, and every single one of them sparkles with an eerie blue glow. Of course, it's not just the glow that gives them away as ghosts, it's also the fact they're all semi-transparent.

You freeze in your tracks, an icy bolt of fear shooting through your body as you realize what you've stumbled upon. It's fascinating to observe, but as someone who is not entirely familiar with the spirit world, you're not sure what will happen should they catch you.

This isn't a question that you have for long, however.

Suddenly, one of the ghostly dancers, a woman in a long white dress, turns and approaches you. She's smiling wide, an expression that you can't seem to place as either sinister or inviting. One thing's for sure, though, the ghost is not at all alarmed to see you. It makes you wonder if she'd known you were hiding there the whole time.

"What are you doing here?" she demands to know, suddenly making her feelings very clear. "How dare you disturb the good people of Home of Truth."

"I'm just..." you stammer, backing away as you shake your head from side to side. "I'm just passing through."

"A simple detour on your way to San Diego?" she hisses. "Is that all we are to you?"

"No!" you blurt.

Suddenly, the ghost's expression changes, softening into a face of good natured laughter. "I'm just messing with you," she offers. "I'm so sorry. There's not much to do when you're a ghost, so scaring people kinda becomes a habit."

"Oh," you reply in startled amazement, deeply thankful for this tonal shift. "Yeah, I bet. How'd you know I was headed to San Diego?"

"Ghosts have a strange relationship with timelines," she explains. "We're here now, but we can see into the past sometimes, or the future, or the potential."

"That's very confusing," you admit.

The ghostly woman nods. "I know. Some stuff will make sense before you ride the lonesome train, some stuff will make sense after, but you should rarely mix the two. For instance, I shouldn't tell you there's a secret compartment in the back of your truck with a device that will alter the very course of history."

"Wait, what?" you blurt.

The phantom's eyes go wide. "Oops."

"Are you serious?" you continue.

The ghost nods. "Yes, but you'll never find it without help so don't even look. Just trust me, it's very important that your package reaches its destination."

This is all a lot to take in, so instead of responding you find yourself falling into an awkward silence as your mind swims in a sea of new information.

"You wanna dance?" the ghost questions, pulling you back to reality.

Decline her offer on page 99
Accept her offer on page 8

130

While you might be able to get these repairs done in other circumstances, crushed halfway into a snowdrift is not ideal.

With this in mind, you decide to hike back up to the shop and see if you can get some help. You make sure the truck is locked up, then begin your journey back up the icy road, taking your time as you struggle to avoid a fall.

Eventually, you arrive back at the gas station. You approach the shop and find the stegosaurs is still there manning his register.

"Hey there," you offer, stepping through the door as a bell rings. "Looks like you were right."

The dinosaur nods. "Yep."

"Brakes were cut," you continue. "I'm down the hill a ways, crashed into a snow drift. I think I can back the truck out of there, but without any brakes I'm screwed."

The scaly prehistoric creature nods along, following your words carefully. "Well, it would've been a lot cheaper to have me check it out before you left," the stegosaurus reminds you.

"I know," you offer in return, not sure what else to say.

The dinosaur takes a deep breath, meditating on this for a moment and then quickly switching gears. He claps his claws together. "Tell you what. I'll fix your truck, but it'll cost you a bit more. What're you carrying in that cargo hold?"

"Chocolate milk," you explain. "This is an important shipment, though. I'm not authorized to give any away."

The stegosaurus glances over at the door between the convenience store and his auto repair garage, looking the space over before returning his attention to you.

"I'm low on spare truck tires," the dinosaur continues. "If you want me to fix your truck, I'll take your spare along with my normal fee."

Agree and offer up the spare truck tire on page 78
Decline and fix it yourself on page 60

"I'm sorry," you tell the dinosaur one last time. "I'm still not interested."

The stegosaurus just stares at you for a moment, then shrugs and turns around to make his way back up the hill. "Suit yourself," he calls out as he continues onward. "I'm tired of watching your back anyway."

When the dinosaur finally disappears you return your attention to the truck, climbing up onto the bumper and peering down inside once again.

"You've got this," you whisper under your breath, trying your best to keep a positive outlook in this completely sideways situation.

Before you have a chance to dive back in, however, you feel a sharp pain in your back. You glance behind you to find that a jackalope has crept through the snow and attacked you by surprise, plunging his enormous sharpened antlers deep into your flesh.

You try to cry out, but your lungs simply refuse to fill with enough air to form the words. Instead, you're left gasping and gurgling, struggling to maintain your composure.

"We just can't take any chances," the jackalope offers in his bizarre sing-song cadence. "Sorry."

You try verbally replying once again, but the ability continues to evade you.

Eventually, you find yourself simply too weak to maintain this position, and soon enough the creature is slipping you off of its antlers and laying you out in the cold snow. Your vision fading, you glance around to see more and more of the enormous rabbit-like creatures bounding into your field of vision.

You watch as the jackalopes begin to unload your truck, passing down the crates of chocolate milk and then carrying them off over the nearby snow drift.

Your eyelids heavy, you gradually drift off into a deep, deep sleep.

THE END

The logical part of your brain knows that you should probably stay focused on the task at hand, but there's something about this bizarre, dancing illumination that takes hold of your curiosity and simply refuses to let go.

You climb out of your cab and lock up the truck, then begin your journey out into the tall grass. Your eyes quickly begin to adjust to the night, and while you still need to maintain a careful, slow pace, you do a pretty good job of getting where you're going. Fortunately, there's not much out here in the middle of nowhere for you to trip over or run into.

As you grow closer and closer to the light, you begin to hear the sweet sound of music floating out across the plains. It's an upbeat song played on fiddle, banjo and guitar, but there's also something distinctly haunting and melancholy about it.

Soon enough, you find yourself at the edge of a small ghost town, a collection of old wooden buildings set in the dirt around a central square, and not much else. The square is populated by several figures, however, and you gasp when you see them.

It appears there's a party going on, with singing and dancing abound. The revelers are all clad in old clothing, like settlers from way back when, and every single one of them sparkles with an eerie blue glow. Of course, it's not just the glow that gives them away as ghosts, it's also the fact they're all semi-transparent.

You freeze in your tracks, an icy bolt of fear shooting through your body as you realize what you've stumbled upon. It's fascinating to observe, but as someone who is not entirely familiar with the spirit world, you're not sure what will happen should they catch you.

This isn't a question that you have for long, however.

Suddenly, one of the ghostly dancers, a woman in a long white dress, turns and approaches you slowly. She's smiling wide, an expression that you can't seem to place as either sinister or inviting. One thing's for sure, though, the ghost is not at all alarmed to see you. It makes you wonder if she'd known you were there the whole time.

"What are you doing here?" she demands to know, suddenly making her feelings very clear. "How dare you disturb the good people of Home of Truth."

"I'm just..." you stammer, backing away as you shake your head from side to side. "I'm just passing through."

"A simple detour on your way to San Diego?" she hisses. "Is that all we are to you?"

"No!" you blurt.

Suddenly, the ghost's expression changes, softening into a face of good natured laughter. "I'm just messing with you," she offers. "I'm so sorry. There's not much to do when you're a ghost, so scaring people kinda becomes a habit."

"Oh," you reply in startled amazement, deeply thankful for this tonal shift. "Yeah, I bet. How'd you know I was headed to San Diego?"

"Ghosts have a strange relationship with timelines," she explains. "We're here now, but we can see into the past sometimes, or the future, or the potential."

"That's very confusing," you admit.

The ghostly woman nods. "I know. Some stuff will make sense before you ride the lonesome train, some stuff will make sense after, but you should rarely mix the two. For instance, I shouldn't tell you that you're actually just a character in a book."

"Wait, what?" you blurt.

"Oops. Nevermind," the phantom blurts, her eyes going wide.

She takes a moment to collect herself as the two of you stand in awkward silence.

"Anyway, you wanna dance?" the ghostly woman questions.

Decline on page 99
Accept on page 8

Your initial instinct is to turn and run, but as you stare down the barrel of this frightening red laser, you remind yourself that you're in no position to disobey the dinosaur's commands.

You put your hands in the air, surrendering to the triceratops.

"Hand over the bag," the dinosaur continues.

"I can't do that," you retort, not sure what else to say.

"Hand over the bag," the dinosaur repeats, this time a little louder.

You take a deep breath and let it out, fully accepting the fact that your options are limited at the moment. You can always get The Big Red Button back once all this is sorted out, but you'll be no use protecting the device is you get yourself vaporized.

You step forward a bit with your arms outstretched, handing over your bag and the bounty within.

The triceratops glances inside, the nods. "Okay, start walking," he announces, motioning toward the distant hill.

You begin to trek deeper into the desert, past the security outpost and into this restricted area.

Behind you, the prehistoric creature turns his head to the side a bit, speaking directly into a microphone on his suit as his gaze remains steadfast.

"Yeah, we have an intruder at the north gate," he says. "Gonna bring them in now. They've got something you're gonna wanna see."

You walk for quite a while, but as you crest over the top of the hill your destination becomes clear. Stretching out below you is an enormous military base, featuring several hangers and a dozen or so airstrips. Sitting on the runways are a variety of different vessels, each one of them unlike anything you've ever seen.

"This... looks like Area 51," you observe, unable to help yourself.

"Oh yeah?" the triceratops scoffs. "You ever *seen* Area 51?"

You shake your head. "I mean, it's what I'd assume Area 51 looks like."

"You really think the government would let everyone know where their alien technology is kept? Area 51 is just a distraction. It's there to keep everyone from looking for Area 52."

Eventually, you find yourself sitting in a sterile white interrogation room.

There's another chair across from you, and a table that rests between. On the wall to your left is a one way mirror, allowing any mysterious observers on the other side to remain anonymous.

You've been waiting here for an hour or so when suddenly the door opens up, a tall, handsome figure standing in the doorway.

"I'm so sorry about that," a green velociraptor in a sharply pressed uniform offers. "We just had to make sure you we're a scoundrel or a devil."

"I'm not," you assure the handsome prehistoric creature.

"I know, I'm sorry," he repeats with deep sincerity. "My name is Captain Orion, I'm the head of the base here at Area 52."

"Are you going to interrogate me?" you question.

The raptor shakes his head. "No, I'm gonna thank you. Come on."

The dinosaur motions for you to stand up and you follow his instructions. Soon enough, the two of you are strolling down the hallway of this hustling, bustling military base, the conversation taking on an unexpected air of comfort.

"We've been in contact with Truckman," Orion explains. "We know all about The Big Red Button and we're here to help."

"Oh, whoa," you blurt, thrilled with this amazing news.

You leave the hallway and suddenly find yourself in one of the enormous airplane hangars. Before you hovers a strange, oval ship, shimmering with extraterrestrial energy as a variety of technicians prepare it for launch.

"All of this alien technology is being studied and integrated in an effort to protect this timeline," Captain Orion explain. "Thusly, your mission is also *our* mission. We want you to deliver The Big Red Button safely."

The raptor turns to a nearby table, picking up your bag and handing it back to you.

"Thank you," you reply, looking inside and finding that the device is, in fact, still there.

"We'll give you a ride to San Diego in one of our ships," Captain Orion explains, then nods toward the strange floating oval. "That one over there. Normal planes will pressurize the device too much, destroying it instantly, but not our ships."

There's a strange, pulsing hum as a ramp slowly unfurls from the belly of the craft.

"Welcome aboard," Orion offers, motioning you toward the vessel.

You walk up the ramp into a brilliantly lit room with no controls or windows. The second you reach the center of this empty space, the ramp begins to close, sealing you inside.

"Wait!" you cry out. "Is there a pilot? How do I fly this thing?"

Someone must have heard you crying out because the ramp begins to lower once again. Strangely, however, the smooth cement floor of the airplane hangar seems to have disappeared.

As you walk down the ramp once more you suddenly realize that you've arrived at your destination. You're right by the water in a deserted industrial section of the San Diego wharf, the endless ocean stretching out to your right while a large warehouse sits waiting on your left.

"We can't protect you once you head inside," the voice of Captain Orion says telepathically, vibrating through your mind. "To keep a low profile, we've gotta head back to the base before anyone else knows we're here."

"Thanks for the ride," you offer, feeling strange as you speak out loud to someone who is communicating through thoughts.

The silver oval rises up off the ground a bit, then suddenly disappears without so much as a sound, vanishing just as quickly as it arrived without a shred of fanfare or explanation.

The only noises now are the soft lapping of waves against the shore and the distant call of a lone seagull.

You look down at your phone, reminding yourself of the scientist that you're looking for. Truckman has sent you a photograph, and you read the name below it aloud to yourself.

"Borson Reems," you say, taking in this middle-aged man's enormous white beard and round nose. He has a kindness in his expression that is truly something to behold.

You bag gripped tight, you walk toward the enormous oceanside warehouse, strolling up to the door and pushing it open.

"Hello?" you call out, your voice echoing across the cavernous space of this wide open industrial building. The ceilings are high and the floor is all cement, giving the space a very specific sonic texture.

There's no response, so you creep in a little more.

"Borson?" you call out, gazing up at the birds perched above on a high metal beam.

"Yes!" comes a jovial voice from around the corner.

Soon enough, Borson Reems is stepping into view. He's a short, stout man with brilliant blue eyes and red cheeks. While he's currently working as a scientist, you've heard from Truckman that he spends most of his time out on the water as a fisherman.

The two of you step toward one another, Borson reaching out toward you in an attempt to take the bag, but suddenly you stop in your tracks.

There was a distinct kindness and soul that was apparent in your photo of Borson, but now that he's standing before you, that inner light seems to be missing for some reason. You feel incredibly silly about your hesitation, but you just can't help yourself.

"Are you alright?" Borson Reems questions.

"Yeah, I'm fine," you stammer, struggling to parse through the unexpected feeling of danger that has suddenly overwhelmed your senses.

You shake your head, rattling your mind back into alignment. This has been a long, harrowing journey, so it's no wonder the promise of a peaceful resolution has made you skeptical.

However, now that you're made it to the end, you shouldn't talk yourself out of crossing the finish line. You don't want to be your own worst enemy.

"Do you have the button?" Borson questions.

You nod.

"Then hand it over!" he cries out, growing frustrated. "There's not much time! Ted Cobbler could be here any minute!"

Hand over The Big Red Button on page 88
If you hesitate, turn to page 142

138

Your first instinct is to make a run for it.

You turn abruptly and begin to sprint off in the other direction, back into the desert from which you came.

Unfortunately, you only get a few steps before the springy blast of the unicorn's laser erupts in your ears. You don't even have time to cry out in shock as your entire body erupts in a burst of flame and viscera, splattering across the sand.

THE END

Finally, you make your choice, handing over The Big Red Button to Borson Reems.

"Thank you," the man replies warmly, softening up a bit.

This expression of warmth doesn't last long however. Soon enough, Borson begins to laugh, a hearty chuckle bubbling up from deep within him and spilling out of his throat in an uncontrollable fit. He's cackling now, and as his vocalizations change, so does his face.

The man standing before you is no longer Borson Reems, but the devilish Ted Cobbler himself.

You attempt to lunge at the bright red creature but before you can, an enormous bigfoot emerges from the shadows behind you, wrapping his hairy arms around your body and holding you tight.

"Let go!" you cry out.

"You've been a thorn in our side for far too long," Ted announces gleefully.

The strength of the bigfoot is far too much to fight back against, and soon enough you find yourself bound by a heavy rope. The one-eyed bigfoot is exceptionally skilled at tying knots, rendering you completely helpless and then hoisting you up over his shoulder.

"No, wait!" you cry out, but the creature is on a mission now, completely ignoring your pleas.

Ted waves goodbye as you're carried out of the warehouse, the one-eyed bigfoot lumbering down a long wooden dock that extends out into the bay. In any other part of the city someone might be able to hear your cries, but in this abandoned industrial sector there's not a soul in sight.

As you reach the end of the dock you make your final case, begging the bigfoot to let you go. "Don't do this!" you cry out. "You may be a scoundrel, but you're not a devil."

"That's what you think," the one-eyed bigfoot replies, then hurls you off the end of the pier and into the icy cold water.

Your limbs bound tight, there's nothing you can do as you sink to the bottom, disappearing into the cold darkness below.

THE END

140

Despite the deep internal desire to make good time, you decide the best and safest idea is to stop in Las Vegas for the evening.

The sparkling lights of the city grow larger and larger as you continue onward, blossoming out before you until they completely fill your vision with dancing bulbs and flickering neon signs.

You pull off the freeway and soon enough you find yourself rolling down the Las Vegas Strip, gazing up in wonder at an assortment of enormous themed hotels. You see one that's designed like a futuristic space station called The Zorbus, and another featuring a lifelike backdrop of The Tinglewood Hills. Eventually, however, you come upon the glorious sight of a giant, waving cowboy who beacons you onward to The Grand Buckaroo Hotel And Casino.

You pull into one of the back parking lots that's big enough to host your rig, then climb out. You double and triple check that you've got your bag with you, The Big Red Button sitting safely inside, then stroll into the lobby in search of a room.

The second you enter this majestic building you find your senses assaulted by buzzers and chimes, an endless ringing calling out to you from the casino floor. There are revelers everywhere, people enjoying their night out in Sin City as they drink chocolate milk and gamble with reckless abandon.

You approach the front desk, greeted warmly by a pterodactyl in a black dress.

"Looking for a room?" she questions.

You nod. "Just one night, please."

The dinosaur types a few things into her computer. "No problem at all," she offers.

Moments later you're handing over some money in exchange for a key. "The pool and garden are located down here on the first floor, our gym is available on the third floor. Check out is at eleven tomorrow morning."

"Thank you," you reply, starting to turn away.

"Oh!" the pterodactyl suddenly calls out, stopping you in your tracks. "We're also currently hosting The World Series Of Blackjack," she explains. "In purchasing the room, you've been randomly selected for complimentary entry."

The dinosaur hands you a coupon card.

"Thank you," you reply, turning it over in your hand.

The dinosaur moves on and begins to help the next customer, but you're frozen in place. Your mission was to stay focused and get some rest, but suddenly an opportunity has presented itself.

What's the harm in trying your hand at some blackjack before hitting the hay?

Just go to bed on page 155
Hit the blackjack tables on page 64

"No," you state flatly, backing away and clutching your bag tight.

Borson's face contorts angrily, the initial friendly nature of this man now slipping away completely to reveal something ghastly underneath.

Suddenly, there's a loud clatter as a figure tumbles out of the nearby closet, bound with rope and gagged by a rag over their mouth. It's another Borson Reems, although now you're fairly certain this is the real man who is seeking your delivery.

The imposter immediately gives up his act, the face of Borson melting away and transforming into the horrific, bright red visage of Ted the devil. Before you have a chance to do anything, he extends his claw forward and strikes you with a powerful, magical pain wave, causing a cry of agony to escape your throat as you collapse to your knees.

Ted's eyes go wide with excitement while he continues to blast you, clearly enjoying the immense display of suffering before him, but he's not at all prepared for what you do next.

Using all the will power you can muster, you reach into your bag and pull out The Big Red Button. "I'll smash it!" you scream.

The devil before you immediately stops.

Moments later, you see the one-eyed bigfoot emerge from a patch of shadows nearby and rush toward you, hoping to catch you off guard. He fails spectacularly as you raise The Big Red Button even higher, acknowledging his presence with a ferocious cry. "Not another step! I'll do it!"

The bigfoot stops, exchanging worried glances with Ted.

"You wouldn't dare," the devil finally offers with a laugh. "You need that device to open up more love based timelines."

"I might not be able to open up timelines of love if I smash this," you retort, "but at least *you* won't be able to open up timelines of hate. Besides, losing The Big Red Button doesn't keep us from proving love the old fashioned way, with kindness and support and care for your fellow buds."

Ted can tell that you're serious, so he backs off a bit, reassessing his options. Gradually, however, a terrifying grin creeps its way across his face.

"I just realized something," Ted offers manically. "I don't really care."

He raises his hand toward you once more, but before he has a chance to cast another spell he explodes in a comically gruesome blast of guts and flame, popping like a balloon and splattering everywhere.

You jump back in shock, then turn your attention to the one-eyed bigfoot who's just as confused as you are. Moments later, he explodes as well.

Footsteps begin to ring out through the warehouse as an assortment of dinosaur space troops in shiny tactical gear reveal their positions, running into the building and greeting you with a salute.

Captain Orion emerges from the bunch with a smile, happy to see you again.

"I thought you had to leave!" you blurt.

The space raptor laughs. "We only pretended to leave so as to avoid any battles that might draw unwanted attention. It seemed like that option was no longer on the table."

You rush over and untie the real Borson Reems, helping him to his feet.

"I have something for you," you offer, proudly handing the scientist his package, The Big Red Button.

"Thank you," Borson gushes. "This is going to change the world. This proves love is real."

The dinosaur space troops begin to chat amongst themselves, satisfied with a job well done.

"You did great," Orion offers, strolling over to you and placing a scaly claw on your shoulder. "It was a real pleasure working with you."

"Likewise," you reply. "Now that I've made my last delivery as a truck driver, I'm gonna miss this kind of adventure."

Captain Orion raises an eyebrow. "So you've got some time on your hands now?" he questions.

You nod.

The raptor smiles a sharp-toothed grin. "How'd you like to join the space squad?"

THE END

144

"This is another scare, isn't it?" you finally reply.

The ghost just laughs. "I was hoping you wouldn't say that, but I knew that you would."

You're not exactly sure what she means, but at this point you're fairly certain this phantom is just messing with you. Regardless, it's time to hit the road.

You say a final goodbye and then turn around, heading back into the wide open field. You're immediately thankful that you didn't fall for the ghost's little prank, realizing just how dangerous it would be to sprint across this wild grassland in the dark. There are holes and dips everywhere, plenty of places to slip an ankle into and quickly find it twisted or broken.

This walk also gives you a little time to appreciate the glorious sky above, gazing up at the stars that shine brilliantly overhead.

Unfortunately, you're so distracted that you don't even notice the giant figure sneaking up behind you in the darkness. The next think you know, two huge, hairy hands are reaching you and grabbing you tight.

`Your immediate instinct is squirm away, kicking and screaming as you fight off this mysterious attacker, but it soon becomes apparent that he's just too strong for you to contend with. The enormous creature begins to carry you back across the field, his muscular arms making it immediately apparent that your unexpected guest is a bigfoot.

From what you can make out, he seems to be wearing a leather jacket and sporting a patch over one eye.

Eventually, you reach the road, where the bigfoot finally sets you down in front of another mysterious stranger.

"Caught him in the field," the bigfoot states gruffly.

You look up to see a bright red devil standing before you, a humanoid figure with stark black hair and two long, curved horns. He has a slender tail with a point at the end, which lashes around his legs as he walks. The devil is wearing a short sleeved button up shirt, and over the heart is a name tag patch that you can just barely make out. It simply reads 'Ted.'

"Where's the device?" the devil demands to know.

"What device?" you question.

"The button," Ted continues sternly.

The ghost was right, you suddenly realize. You should've listened, but now it's too late.

You shake your head profusely. "I don't know, I'm just driving a shipment of chocolate milk. I have no idea what you're talking about."

The devil grins. "Then why is your truck empty?"

"The milk was stolen," You explain desperately.

"But you're still headed toward San Diego, are you not?" Ted continues. "Something doesn't add up here, but it will soon enough."

The bigfoot behind you steps forward a bit, trying his best to be imposing and doing a damn good job. "Should I smash them to bits?" the bigfoot questions.

Ted shakes his head. "Not yet. We might need some help getting this thing open."

Suddenly, the devil thrusts his hands out toward you as a cascade of swirling green energy erupts from his fingertips, wrapping itself around your body and pulling tight. You cry out in surprise as your form begins to change shape, shrinking down and pulling inward as your skin hardens into scale. The sound of your voice morphs into a long hiss, and soon enough you find yourself lying flat in the middle of the road, staring up from a new, much smaller body.

Ted has turned you into a snake.

While these reptiles are quite fast when they want to be, you're too shocked to take any immediate action. Before you get a chance to slither away, the giant bigfoot reaches down and grabs ahold of your long green body, picking you up and dropping you into a bucket.

You open your mouth to cry out, but can't find a way to form the words. Instead, you focus this energy into climbing out and escaping, but the bigfoot swiftly covers the top of your container with a sturdy piece of flat wood.

There's a series of loud clangs and eventually the sound of your truck roaring to life, hotwired up and ready to go. It appears both vehicles are prepped for the journey ahead.

Moments later, the weight of your bucket begins to shift. You're being lifted in the air and carried somewhere, then set down roughly on what you can only assume is a truck bench.

The familiar rumble of a motor beneath your body lets you know that you're on your way.

Continue your journey on page 157

You decide to stay and face these bullies head on, but as the truck stops and the doors open up you quickly begin to wonder if that was such a good idea. You're trying to maintain a confident outlook, but deep down you're absolutely terrified.

From out of the darkness two silhouettes emerge, one much larger than the other. The enormous figure soon reveals himself to be a rather imposing bigfoot, clad in a dark leather jacket and sporting an enormous beard that hangs down the front of his hairy, muscular body. He reveals himself and then stops, hanging back to keep an eye on things as his partner steps forward.

The second backlit figure to emerge from the darkness is a bright red devil, a humanoid figure with stark black hair and two long, curved horns. He has a slender tail with a point at the end, which lashes around his legs as he walks. The devil is wearing a short sleeved button up shirt, and over the heart is a small name tag patch that simply reads 'Ted.'

"Hand over the device," Ted demands, the devils voice drifting across your ears with a deep and menacing tone.

"I have no idea what you're talking about," you reply.

"Go around and look in the back," Ted commands the bigfoot. "I guess our friend won't mind us taking a peek."

As the bigfoot follows Ted's orders you rush to stop him. The second you move, however, the devil reaches out toward you with his clawed red hand. Suddenly, a magical eruption of searing pain overwhelms your body, causing you to cry out loud as you collapse to your knees in agony.

"I wouldn't do that," Ted offers with a gleeful smile, twisting his hand as he continues to pump magical pain waves into your nervous system.

When you've finally had enough, Ted relents, causing you to crumble in an exhausted heap.

Meanwhile, the muscular bigfoot has arrived at the back of your truck and picked up a large rock from the side of the road. He approaches your lock and begins to hammer away at it, slamming his boulder across the metal over and over again until it finally pops open and falls into the gravel with a thud.

The bigfoot throws open the roll up door, then climbs up into the refrigerated cargo hold. The next thing you know, your ears are assaulted by the sound of hundreds of chocolate milk crates being opened up and smashed onto the asphalt road below. The bigfoot is ruthless, tearing through the contents of your truck as you watch in absolute horror.

Ted may have powerful magic at his disposal, but maybe you can fight your way through the pain and somehow stop this bigfoot before he discovers the secret compartment.

Try to stop him on page 114
Talk your way out of this on page 54

148

The longer you stay here, the more impressed you become with your potential options. Even though Baraza has yet to return with her recommended vehicle, there are plenty of things here that will get you at least *part* of the way to San Diego in style. You can't wait to see what she brings back for you to check out.

Now that you think of it, you suddenly realize that the living motorcycle has been gone for quite a while.

Suddenly, a powerful screech erupts from above you, not high up in the sky but directly over your head. You glance up and cry out as an enormous eagle swoops down, soaring past you like a rocket and grabbing onto your bag with its mighty claws.

The creature is breathtakingly powerful, and although you try your best to maintain control of the bag, and the device within, it's no use. There's a sharp tearing sound as the massive bird rips the bag from your hands, taking off into the sky once again.

Panic immediately floods through you. Your entire mission has suddenly found its way into the claws of an enormous bird who is, in all likelihood, already far, far away.

Not knowing what to do, you finally decide to rush even deeper into the junkyard in search of Bazara. Maybe this eagle is a common nuisance around here, or maybe your new friend knows where the predator's nest is located.

You weave in and out of the junk stacks until suddenly emerging next to a shack with the words Baraza's Junk And Salvage written across the top in refurbished metal signage.

Not wasting any time, you rush up the front steps and enter the building.

"Hello?" you cry out. "I need some help!"

This shack is partitioned into two sections, a front office and the back room behind it, but it's small enough for you to immediately recognize that Baraza isn't here. American flags hang everywhere, along with various patriotic paraphernalia that might seem nice in other circumstances, but in this context feels a bit strange. Bazara seems a bit obsessed.

Eventually, your eyes fall onto something that turns your blood to ice. There behind the counter is an enormous bird cage, large enough for an eagle. The door hanging wide open.

As you stare at the cage, mouth agape, you also notice a horrifying bumper sticker that's been slapped against the back of the register. 'Cobbler Trucking,' it reads.

You suddenly realize that this sentient motorcycle is clearly a friend of Ted's, and with the speed of an eagle working against you, your device may have already fallen into the wrong hands.

You turn back around and rush through the door, out into the junkyard once again, but you stop in your tracks when you notice that the morning sky has already changed color before you. The once golden sunrise is mired with streaks of jet black, stretching upward like taffy as it disappears into a massive, looming darkness above.

You watch as pieces of scrap metal and junk begin to float upward, the very fabric of this timeline emitting a horrific groan as it tears down the middle. The building blocks of reality break apart, swept away as existence dissolves into nothingness.

THE END

150

Deciding to take your chances and fix the truck yourself, you maneuver yourself around to the front of the big-rig. It's a large vehicle, but you have no problem getting in there by popping the hood and climbing up onto the front bumper.

From here, you're provided a clear view down into the belly of the beast, immediately noticing that your brake lines have, in fact, been severed. Strangely, it's not a clear cut like you might've expected, but a ragged slice from someone rubbing a hard spike back and forth across the wire.

"Turn around slowly," comes a strange, high-pitched voice from behind you. It has a bizarre sing-song cadence, which gives it an almost gurgling quality.

You do as you're told, turning around slowly to find that you're surrounded by six enormous jackalopes. While you've never seen a jackalope before in real life, you're heard plenty of stories about these giant rabbits with sharp pointy antlers protruding from the top of their heads.

While some claim this society of wild creatures is mischievous and fun, other's describe their actions as downright criminal. It looks like the latter were right.

"Open up the back of the truck," the head jackalope demands, the spikes of his enormous antlers shining bright and sharp.

"No," you reply.

"Open the back of the truck," the creature gurgles again, this time with much more force. The group of jackalopes hop a little closer, closing in their circle around you.

Open the truck on page 34
Refuse on page 73

Clearly there's been some kind of misunderstanding, but you're confident in your ability to clear it up quickly.

"I'll go with you," you offer, "but you've got the wrong person. I'd like to see whatever proof you have."

The unicorns exchange glances and their leader nods in approval. They back off, but not too much, then begin to march you through the casino. Patrons turn and watch you go, whispering to one another about this ominous parade making its way through the rows of green felted table games and humming slot machines.

Eventually, you arrive at a door that gives way to a sterile white hall running the length of the building. This area is for casino personnel only, free from any prying eyes, and the unicorns make use of this fact the second you enter.

Suddenly, one of the creatures is on either side of you, grabbing you firmly by the arms and roughly pulling you along with them.

"Hey! What the hell?" you blurt, angered by this unexpected shift in demeanor.

The squad of unicorns barely pay you a second glance, just continue onward through a maze of hallways and then eventually down some stairs into the belly of the casino. You've already realized that going with them was a terrible choice, but no matter how much you struggle you simply can't break away from the group.

You approach another door and the unicorns throw you through it, following behind as you collapse to the ground. You're significantly roughed up now, and as you struggle to collect your senses you hear a terrifyingly familiar voice drift across your ears.

"Hello there," Ted hisses, the bright red devil sitting in a chair before you. "I see you've brought me The Big Red Button. How kind of you."

The unicorns grab your bag and tear it away, then hand it over to the devil.

Ted pulls out the device and turns it over in his hands, inspecting it with a mischievous smile that grows wider and wider by the second.

"Don't," is all you can think to say. "You can't."

"Oh, but I can," Ted retorts. "Cobbler Enterprises is much more than just a shipping and cargo business. Sure, it started simple enough with Cobbler Trucking, but since then we've moved into media, politics... hell, we've even gotten into the casino industry."

The unicorns start to laugh as you watch in horror. Ted stands up from his table and strolls past you with a wink, waving goodbye with The Big Red Button in his hands. The unicorns follow behind, pushing you back as you make one final attempt to escape.

The next thing you know, the door is closing and locking you in. You pound your fists as hard as you can against the metal, but it's no use. There isn't even cell phone service down here.

Eventually, you end up turning and sliding down the wall in agony. You wait like this for a long, long time, so long that you barely even notice when the fabric of reality begins to split apart.

THE END

You return to the table and sit back down, trying your best to keep up your energy and push across the finish line with just as much confidence as you had at the start of this competition.

"Feeling good?" Keith the jet plane questions.

You nod. "Yeah, I've got this."

Moments later, you see Keith's gaze drift past you, floating over your shoulder and landing on something in the background. His expression quickly changes to one of deep concern and confusion.

"Looks like you've got some visitors," the jet plane offers.

You turn around to see what he's looking at and find a collection of unicorns in dark suits and sunglasses. They're standing at attention as they surround you, the leader of the bunch stepping forward and pulling you to your feet.

"Please come with us," the lead unicorn commands, a bright green and muscular creature.

"No," you blurt. "The competition is starting."

"You can come back and play once we're finished talking," the unicorn security officer assures you.

"What's this about?" you question.

"We have video of you stealing from the casino," the bright green unicorn retorts.

Run away on page 67
Go with the unicorns to page 151

154

You stare out across the San Diego shoreline from the deck of your oceanside hotel, enjoying the beach and the glorious sunset beyond. It's your first night of retirement, and you couldn't be happier. You were hoping for an exciting last ride, after all, and that one certainly fits the bill.

You reach over and grab the glass of ice cold chocolate milk sitting next to you, taking a long, satisfying pull from the sweet and delicious beverage.

This is what it's all about.

As the sound of the ocean hums peacefully in your ears, you kick up your feet and close your eyes, basking in the moment.

Maybe the perfect timeline really *does* exist out there, maybe it doesn't. One thing you do know for sure: you're satisfied with the one you've got.

THE END

As tempting as a night of blackjack sounds, you really should get some sleep.

Instead of heading out onto the casino floor, you make a sharp right turn and head for the elevators, making your way up to your room and then flopping out on the bed in a state of utter exhaustion. You fall asleep laying sprawled out just like this.

Suddenly, you open your eyes, yanked from a deep slumber by the alarming sound of someone trying to force their way into your room. They have a key card, and it seems to have worked, but you had enough sense last night in your tired delirium to use the inside bolt.

Whoever is out there has slammed themselves against the door once, cracking the wood but not splintering it completely. In a matter of seconds, they'll likely try it again.

Thinking fast, you spring off the bed and duck into the bathroom, hiding in the shower as you peer out from a crack in the doorway.

There's a loud bang as the door to your hotel room flies open and a group of unicorns in dark suits and sunglasses start pouring in. Their leader, a particularly muscular unicorn with light green skin, calls out for you.

"We have footage of you stealing from the casino!" he calls out. "You need to come with us."

Unless you were sleepwalking, this couldn't be the case. Something much more sinister is going on here, although you're still not exactly sure what it is.

Once all six of the security guards have filtered into your room you seize the moment, erupting out of the bathroom and making a break for it. You sprint into the hallway, unicorns hot on your heels as you slam into a stairwell door and start making your way downward.

"Stop!" the unicorns are crying out. "Get back here!"

You don't listen, just continue down the stairs as quickly as you can. Your focus in perfectly honed, making sure you don't trip from going too fast, nor go so slow that the security guards catch up with you.

It's not long before you reach the ground floor and burst out into the chaos. You immediately find yourself ducking and dodging through the crowd of gamblers and casino workers, nearly bowling over a waitress who just barely maintains the balance of her chocolate milk tray.

156

Soon enough you're high tailing it through the ringing, chattering casino floor, the flashing slot machines passing by you on either side while the unicorns follow in hot pursuit. You glance back over your shoulder to see a few of them splitting off in either direction, likely attempting to block the exits.

That just means you'll need to kick up the speed a little more.

"Get back here!" the lead security unicorn demands, calling out and shaking his fist in anger.

Your pursuers have a distinct advantage in knowing the layout here, but you manage to catch a glimpse of some hanging signs as they pass you by.

To your left is the casino garden, and to the right is the pool.

Head toward the garden on page 42
Head toward the pool on page 165

Hours pass by as you stay coiled up here in the bottom of the bucket. It's a horrific way to spend your time, trying your best to adjust to the sensations of your new body. You find your tongue will shoot out from your mouth involuntarily, lashing the air before you with its new forked shape. Sometimes you'll think about moving your arms or legs, then suddenly realize you have none to speak of, immediately growing frustrated and scared within your new frame.

Eventually, however, exhaustion overtakes you. Somehow you manage to drift off to sleep, soothed by the familiar rumble of the road below you.

You wake up some time later to the sound of muffled voices.

"Well, I've got the mechanics of the lock figured out, and that's the biggest step," a voice is explaining.

"That's not enough," Ted replies with his unmistakable devilish tone. "Half of a picked lock is still a lock."

"We just need the magic words," the voice continues. "You knock on the compartment three times and then say the phrase. Once we know the phrase, we've got The Big Red Button."

"And you have a spell for that?" Ted continues.

"A ritual," the voice explains. "It'll take a bit longer, but we'll know the password by sundown."

It's hard to tell exactly where these voices are coming from in relation to your bucket, but with your new snake body there's all kinds of unexpected information coming your way. Your hearing is complimented by a distinct vibrational sense, the faint movement of feet across a floor and a strange hum emitting from one of the entities.

You get the distinct impression that Ted is talking to a sentient motorcycle, and that the two of them are in an adjacent room.

Now that you're alone, you realize you might be able to tip the bucket over and make your escape. Of course, your snake senses are not entirely reliable and still a little difficult to interpret. You wouldn't be surprised to find these voice are actually emitting from right next to you.

You consider your options, then make your choice.

Rock the bucket on page 200
Wait for a better moment on page 197

Remembering that you've got a lucky unicorn shoe, you pull it out and give the metal semi-circle a rub with your fingers, hoping to brush off a little of the magic for yourself.

Who knows if it actually works.

You sit back down at the blackjack table just in time for the game to start up again, the cards coming out and everyone taking a look at what they've got. There's a slight gasp when you your two cards are revealed.

"Blackjack," the dealer announces, handing you your winnings.

Surely this must be a coincidence, you think, but after the next few hands you begin to think that your lucky unicorn shoe might be working a lot harder than you initially thought.

Gradually, the other players start to bust out, eventually dropping the field down to just you and Keith the jet plane.

"I've gotta say, and I mean this in the nicest way possible, but you're the luckiest person I've ever met," Keith informs you. "You've been on a hell of a run."

"Thanks," you reply, not knowing what else to say.

"How'd you like to join my card counting team?" the sentient vehicle questions. "You wouldn't even need to know the count with luck like this."

"It sounds nice," you admit, "but I'm on a mission. I shouldn't even be here right now."

Keith narrows his eyes in confusion. "What do you mean?"

You lower your voice a bit, despite the fact there's only two of you left at the table. You hesitate for only a moment, then succumb to the trust that you've gradually developed for your new jet plane friend.

"I'm in the process of delivering a device that has the power to destroy or save the world," you explain. "It's called The Big Red Button, and I need to get it to a scientist in San Diego as soon as possible."

Keith laughs. "Why didn't you say so? I know a bunch of planes at the San Diego Airport! Let's just bring the scientist to you."

"You'd do that?" you blurt, blown away by his helpful generosity.

The jet plane shrugs. "I mean, the fate of the world depends on it right?"

The dealer suddenly interrupts your conversation, motioning toward Keith. "Would you like to hit or stand?" he questions.

"I don't care," Keith replies.

"You need to choose, sir," the dealer continues.

The jet plane shrugs, amused. "I quit then, give my friend here the grand prize."

Your eyes go wide. "Wait, what?" you blurt.

"It's fine," Keith explains "I'm a billionaire already. I just do The World Series Of Blackjack for fun."

Alarm bells start going off as confetti begins to fall from the ceiling above you.

"We have a winner!" the dealer announces, springing to his feet.

You stand at attention in the wide open expanse of the Las Vegas Airport, a tarmac nearby and the recently landed plane from Santa Monica finally rolling to a stop.

You glace over at Keith, who is right there with you, and offer one last "thank you."

"Don't mention it," the jet plane replies. "This timeline is important to all of us."

You turn back to see that a short, stout man is emerging from his vehicle, climbing down a set of stairs and then making his way toward you with a wide smile and open arms. He sports round features and a friendly smile that's buried beneath a large white beard.

"Hello! Hello!" the man calls out as he greets you with a hug.

"You must be Borson Reems," you offer.

"In the flesh," the scientist responds.

You pull out your bag and hand it over to him. Borson immediately looks inside, a sense of wonder and amazement overwhelming his expression. "The Big Red Button," he gushes aloud.

Borson reaches in and carefully pulls out the device, turning it over in his hands as he inspects the intricate nature of this machine.

"Thank you for keeping this out of the wrong hands," the scientist offers with a deep sincerity, turning his attention back to you. "This will unlock more than just the secrets of timeline transportation, it will unlock the potential for more love in this universe than we ever thought possible."

Borson pauses again, lost in thought, then suddenly returns to reality.

"I better get started!" he announces. "I'm headed to a secret facility in the desert where I'll be safe to do my work: Area 52."

You say your goodbyes. Moments later, Borson Reems is rushing over to a fleet of black, unmarked SUVs, leaving just as quickly as he arrived.

As you watch Borson take off into the wide open Nevada desert, Keith turns his attention back to you, an inquisitive look on his jet plane face.

"So what are you gonna do now?" the billionaire jet plane questions. "The card counting team offer still stands."

Become a card counter on page 31
If you still love trucking, turn to page 186

You decide to trust the sentient corn and accept her ride, running around the car and opening up the passenger side door to climb in and take your seat. Despite all this, you still remember to keep The Big Red Button close, never letting the bag out of your sight.

"I'm Michelle," the corn offers. "It's nice to meet you."

"Thanks for the ride," you reply. "I guess it would've been quite the walk to San Diego had I turned you down."

The living food laughs. "Thank you! I like the company. So why are you traveling to California?"

You hesitate before answering, struggling to think of some realistic lie on the spot and completely blowing it. There's clearly a moment of awkwardness.

"That's okay," the sentient corn continues. "We'll have plenty more to talk about on the way."

"Why are you going to Las Vegas?" you question, thankful Michelle is letting you off the hook.

"The World Series Of Blackjack," the beautiful yellow and green corn cob announces. "I've got a good feeling about this year."

You're immediately intrigued by her response. While time is clearly limited on this trip, the thought of entering a competition like this one sounds like an absolute blast. You're a little jealous of the way your journeys will soon diverge.

"What's the grand prize?" you question.

"A billion dollar sportscar," Michelle replies.

The two of you spend the rest of the day chatting and enjoying each other's company, watching as the plains transition into mountains and valleys and eventually the endless desert of Nevada. For a brief moment you actually forget the insanity of your trip thus far, and the danger that lies ahead. Instead, you simply enjoy the present with your new friend.

The sun creeps slowly across the sky overhead, starting on one side and gradually ending up on the other. You've been making amazing time, and as it begins to set again you see the shimmering lights of Las Vegas come into view.

"You should enter The World Series Of Blackjack with me," Michelle suddenly offers, glancing over at you with an excited grin. "Wouldn't that be fun?"

"I really can't stop in Vegas," you reply.

162

"Well, technically, you *have* to stop," the sentient corn reminds you. "At least until you find your next ride."

She's got a point. No matter what, you'll be pausing in Vegas, you might as well enjoy your time there. Not only that, but it sounds like the sports car grand prize could offer you some unexpected transportation on the next leg of your journey.

Of course, you'd have to win for that plan to work, and winning requires entering. Entering requires money.

"I don't know if I can afford it," you finally reply.

The sentient corn hesitates for a second, then finally finishes her thought with an invitation. "I'll cover you," she offers.

"What?" you blurt, deeply flattered by unable to accept. "No. I couldn't ask you to do that."

"Please," she continues, the tone of her voice becoming firm and direct. "You've kept me company this whole way. I really appreciate it, and I'd like to return the favor."

"I can't," you start, but before you get a chance to finish, the living vegetable is shaking her head and holding up a hand.

"I don't wanna hear it," Michelle barrels onward. "It's my treat. You're entering this competition."

Accept her invitation on page 12
Decline and keep moving on page 56

You immediately spring into action, taking off into the grass at a full sprint. Soon enough, you're enveloped in the darkness of the night, hidden away as you watch from afar.

It appears the occupants of this other vehicle are more interested in your truck than they are you, as they refuse to give chase. Instead, two figures slowly walk out into their own headlights, talking amongst themselves as the they formulate a plan.

You can't make out their words from all the way over here, but you do manage to get a good look at the frightening characters. The first is a tall and rather imposing bigfoot, clad in a dark leather jacket and sporting an enormous beard that hangs down the front of his hairy, muscular body. He also has a patch over one eye.

The second backlit figure to emerge from the darkness is a bright red devil, a humanoid figure with stark black hair and two long, curved horns. He has a slender tail with a point at the end, which lashes around his legs as he walks. The devil is wearing a short sleeved button up shirt, and over the heart is a name tag patch that you can just barely make out. It simply reads 'Ted.'

After a bit of discussion the bigfoot strolls around to the back of your truck. He picks up a large rock from the side of the road and smashes open the lock, then rolls up the door to your cargo hold with a loud rattle.

Next, the bigfoot climbs up into the back of the truck and begins to search around, stomping from one end of the refrigerated container to the other. Without any chocolate milk back there, the truck is much easier to search, but it's also more suspicious to find completely empty.

"The device isn't here," the bigfoot eventually calls out.

"What?" Ted erupts angrily. "This is the truck! It has to be there!"

The devil now springs into action, making his way around to the back of the truck and having a look for himself. The two of them continue their search, growing more and more frustrated by the second.

As someone spying from afar, this frustration only helps your cause. Their tone is much louder now, heightened to a point that you can easily hear them.

"There must be a secret door!" Ted cries out. "There's magic brewing!"

"You know magic, though," the bigfoot retorts. "You can dispel it!"

164

"Not this powerful!" Ted continues, his voice bubbling over with absolute rage. "Find the driver! They must know the way in!"

The two figures hop down from the back of your truck. "You go that way and I'll go this way," you hear the bright red devil instruct, the two of them splitting off in either direction to search the field.

Fortunately, neither one of them is wandering your direction yet, and there's plenty of ground for them to cover. If you stay here long enough, they'll certainly find you, but at least you've got a moment to think.

At this point, a few courses of action come to mind.

With a spare tire you could sneak over there and quickly make the repair, then drive off as fast as possible.

Of course, you could also just make a run for it, but the longer these two have your truck in their possession, the more likely they are to discover the secret compartment.

Maybe you could creep over there and find the item for yourself, stealing it away before the devil and the bigfoot get a chance to take it?

If you have a spare truck tire and want to put it on, then drive away, turn to page 5
Make a run for it on page 32
Sneak over and search for the secret item yourself on page 180

You make a fast break for the pool, sprinting down one last leg of slot machines and then erupting out onto the deck of a wild party. There are revealers everywhere, enjoying this hot Las Vegas night half-submerged in the cool water of an enormous pool while a band rocks out on a floating platform nearby. You immediately recognize the song they're playing as 'Love Is Real!' by Martha Moobin, one of your favorite tracks, and it mentally allows you to kick things into an even higher gear.

"We love you, Martha!" screams a fan as they wave excitedly, then dive into the pool with a resounding splash.

The chaos of this poolside atmosphere is the perfect cover for your getaway, and you don't take it for granted as you slip into the crowd. You keep your head down and creep along through the pool party, glancing up every once in a while to get a read on the unicorns as they fan out and make their search.

"Great party, huh?" a handsome bigfoot shouts over the music, raising his chocolate milk in your direction. "The name's Torbo Gulgot! I'm here for the sommelier convention! What about you?"

You offer a silent head shake, declining his introduction. You're flattered by the fact this creature is hoping to strike up a conversation, but still trying your best to keep a low profile.

You continue onward when suddenly run directly into a unicorn security guard who grabs you by the shoulders and immediately begins to radio the others.

"I found the target! I found the target!" he's yelling into a microphone on his collar, struggling to get his voice up over the powerful vocals of Martha Moobin.

Thinking fast, you shove the unicorn as hard as you can. He stumbles back, struggling to catch himself and then slipping on the edge of the pool. He lands in the water with an enormous splash. The whole crowd cheers, which would be wonderful if not for the fact that all eyes are on you now, including those of the unicorn security team.

You break out into a sprint once again, pushing partiers out of the way and eventually reaching the other side of the pool deck. Here you find a lone exit door, then dash through it to emerge in a back alley.

"That way!" the lead unicorn security guard cries out.

With no time to waste, you run down the alleyway and make a sharp turn onto Las Vegas Boulevard.

166

The lights of the city greet you once again, cars whizzing past as the neon signs twinkle above. You glance back over your shoulder to see the troop of angry unicorns hot on your tail, slowly but surely closing the distance.

You realize now that it's only a matter of time before you get caught, and in this moment the only thing that can save you is luck. Fortunately, that's exactly what this city is known for.

If you have a lucky unicorn shoe or a lucky jackalope's foot turn to page 83
If you have no lucky items turn to page 192

"No," you state flatly, backing up and clutching your bag tight.

Borson's face contorts angrily, the initial friendly nature of this man now slipping away to reveal something ghastly underneath.

Suddenly, there's a loud clatter as a figure tumbles out of the nearby closet, bound with rope and gagged by a rag over their mouth. It's another Borson Reems, although this time you're fairly certain this is the real man who seeks your delivery.

The imposter immediately gives up his act, the face of Borson melting away and transforming into the horrific, bright red visage of Ted the devil. Before you have a chance to do anything, he brings his claw forward and hits you with a powerful, magical pain wave, causing a cry of agony to escape your throat as you collapse to your knees.

Ted's eyes go wide with excitement as he continues to blast you, clearly enjoying the immense display of suffering before him. However, he's not at all prepared for what you do next.

Using all the will power you can muster, you reach into your bag and pull out The Big Red Button. "I'll smash it!" you scream.

The devil before you immediately stops.

Moments later, you see the one-eyed bigfoot emerge from a patch of shadows nearby and rush toward you, hoping to catch you off guard. He fails spectacularly as you raise The Big Red Button even higher, acknowledging his presence with a ferocious cry. "Not another step! I'll do it!"

The bigfoot stops, exchanging worried glances with Ted.

"You wouldn't dare," the devil finally offers with a laugh. "You need that device to open up more love based timelines."

"I might not be able to open up timelines of love if I smash this," you retort, "but at least *you* won't be able to open up timelines of hate. Besides, losing The Big Red Button doesn't keep us from proving love the old fashioned way, with kindness and support and care for your fellow buds."

Ted can tell that you're serious, so he backs off a bit, reassessing his options. The two of you stand in this face off for quite a while, neither one of you making a move as you wait for the other to falter in some drastic way that never arrives.

Eventually, the real Borson Reems speaks ups, having finally ungagged himself by chewing through the rag and somehow pulling it to the side with his teeth. "Let them go," the scientist demands. "I've already gotten a good look at The Big Red Button. I can build you a new one just from seeing it, but I'll only do that if you let them go."

Ted scoffs. "I believe you're a smart guy, but not that smart."

"I can build another Big Red Button," Borson repeats sternly, a potent look of conviction in his eyes. "I just need my supplies. The hardest part is the external trigger mechanism, the piece that keeps the button stable. Now that I've gotten a good look at it, I'm certain I can build one myself."

You can't let this go on any longer. "What are you doing?" you interrupt.

"It's okay," Borson replies, a mighty weight in his voice. "Just get out of here."

Ted clears his throat. "Okay, fine," the devil says. "I'm sick of standing here so... you've got yourself a deal."

You glance down at Borson, who is still tied to his chair. He mouths the words 'it's okay.'

Soon enough, the one-eyed bigfoot is walking over and lifting up Borson Reems, then freeing him from the chair. Borson begins to rush this way and that, going through his supply cabinets as he searches for various tools.

"The authorities could be here any second," Ted goads. "Get your supplies and let's go."

Your freedom promised, you turn around and run out of the warehouse. You've escaped, but the fresh sea air hitting your skin isn't nearly as satisfying as you'd hoped.

There's gotta be something more you can do. It can't just end like this.

If you have the devil keys turn to page 190
If you don't have the devil keys turn to page 204

You immediately spring into action, taking off into the grass at a full sprint. Soon enough, you're enveloped in the darkness of the night, hidden away as you watch from afar.

It appears the occupants of this other vehicle are more interested in your truck than they are you, as they refuse to give chase. Instead, two figures slowly walk out into their own headlights, talking amongst themselves as the they formulate a plan.

You can't make out their words from all the way over here, but you do manage to get a good look at the frightening characters. The first is a tall and rather imposing bigfoot, clad in a dark leather jacket and sporting an enormous beard that hangs down the front of his hairy, muscular body. He has an eye patch covering one eye.

The second backlit figure to emerge from the darkness is a bright red devil, a humanoid figure with stark black hair and two long, curved horns. He has a slender tail with a point at the end, which lashes around his legs as he walks. The devil is wearing a short sleeved button up shirt, and over the heart is a name tag patch that you can just barely make out. It simply reads 'Ted.'

After a bit of discussion the bigfoot strolls around to the back of your truck. He picks up a large rock from the side of the road and smashes open the lock, then rolls up the door to your cargo hold with a loud rattle.

Next, the bigfoot climbs up into the back of the truck and begins to go through your shipment, tearing open crates of delicious chocolate milk and tossing them out onto the road with a series of horrific smashes and crunches. You watch in absolute disgust as the entire contents of your truck is emptied out before you, all of that glorious chocolate milk gone to waste as it pours across the glass covered ground below.

As the anger within you builds, you seriously consider marching back over there and giving them a piece of your mind, but you muster up all the discipline you can manage and hold yourself back. Something much more important is at play.

"The device isn't here," the bigfoot eventually calls out.

"What?" Ted erupts angrily. "This is the truck! It has to be there!"

The devil springs into action, making his way around to the back of the truck and having a look for himself. The two of them continue to search, growing more and more frustrated by the second.

As someone spying on them from afar, this frustration only helps

170

your cause. Their tone is much louder now, heightened to a point that you can easily hear them.

"There must be a secret door!" Ted cries out. "There's magic brewing!"

"You know magic, though," the bigfoot retorts. "You can dispel it!"

"Not this powerful!" Ted continues, his voice bubbling over with absolute rage. "Find the driver! They must know the way in!"

The two figures hop down from the back of your truck. "You go that way and I'll go this way," you hear the bright red devil instruct, the two of them splitting off in either direction to search the field.

Fortunately, neither one of them is wandering in your exact direction yet, and there's plenty of ground for them to cover. If you stay here long enough, they'll certainly find you, but at least you've got a moment to think.

At this point, a few courses of action come to mind.

With a spare tire you could sneak over there and quickly make the repair, then drive off as fast as possible.

Of course, you could also just make a run for it, but the longer these two have your truck in their possession, the more likely they are to discover the secret compartment.

Maybe you could creep over there and find the item for yourself, stealing it away before the devil and the bigfoot get a chance to take it?

If you have a spare truck tire and want to put it on, then drive away, turn to page 5
Make a run for it on page 32
Sneak over and search for the secret item yourself on page 180

There's no way you can take on all six of these creatures by yourself, and as much as you'd like to fight them off and end this quickly, that just doesn't seem like a good plan.

"Okay," you finally reply.

Your hands in the air, you trudge around to the back of your truck as the creatures follow closely behind with their sharpened antlers at the ready. When you reach the large, roll-up door, you reach into your pocket and pull out the keys, then undo the lock. You grip the bottom of the door and then throw it upward with a loud clatter, revealing a stash of glorious brown chocolate milk crates stacked high within the refrigerated interior.

Suddenly, a loud crack erupts through the wilderness around you, the sound of a gunshot that immediately sends the jackalopes scattering. You duck down instinctively, glancing around to find that the stegosaurus is standing on a nearby snow covered ridge. He's fired into the air, hoping to scare off these creatures with a warning shot and clearly succeeding.

"Go on! Get!" the dinosaur yells out as the jackalopes continue to bound away in every direction.

One of the creatures hops right past you, heading up the road when suddenly an unexpected truck comes barreling around the corner. The jackalope has little time to react, and it's not enough to avoid getting plowed down by the enormous vehicle as it rumbles past. The big-rig doesn't even slow down, just continues on its way.

"Oh my god," you blurt.

You rush over to the creature's side but it's clearly gone, flattened out on the icy asphalt.

The stegosaurus approaches. "You're welcome," he offers.

"I..." you stammer, not quite sure what to say. "Thank you for scaring them off... but..."

The dinosaur glances over your shoulder, checking out the truck. "You sure you don't need any help with that?" he questions. "Once those jackalopes find their buddies, there's gonna be more coming. You should probably take care of business pretty quick."

Maybe he's right. "Same deal?" you question. "The spare tire and some cash?"

"Same deal," the dinosaur replies with a nod.

Trade your spare truck tie for some help on page 63
Fix it yourself on page 131

Thinking fast, you leap over the counter and rush toward the eagle cage. You swiftly tear open the door, throwing it wide and then stepping back as the enormous bird leaps through.

"Be free majestic creature!" you yell triumphantly.

You fully expect the bird to take off in the air with its enormous wings, but instead it lunges directly at you, cutting your words short and transforming them into a frantic shriek. You try your best to cover your face but the creature's talons are too long and its beak is too sharp.

Baraza erupts from the back room, but that's the least of your worries as the giant bald eagle continues to screech and attack.

You stumble backward and collapse to the ground as the bird tears away at your flesh, screaming in pain.

"Looks like you've got yourself a big breakfast!" Baraza cries out excitedly, laughing as you succumb to your wounds and the world around you fades to black.

THE END

174

You're not exactly sure what it is, but there's something about Bazara that you don't quite trust.

The second this sentient motorcycle putters away through the maze of metal wreckage you spring into action, following her closely and keep an eye on this mysterious figure. Chances are you'll discover absolutely nothing sinister, just a kind soul trying to run her strange junkyard in the middle of nowhere, but after the events of last night it's just not worth the risk.

You've gotta stay vigilant.

Eventually, Bazara arrives at a small shack in the middle of the scrapyard. She rolls inside, disappearing from view, which prompts you to quietly run over and hide yourself against the side of this small structure. You creep along the wall then peer into the window carefully.

It appears this building is where Bazara does most of her business. It's decorated with all kinds of patriotic paraphernalia, American flags hanging everywhere and an utterly enormous bald eagle sitting in a cage behind the counter. Beyond this is a back room, where you can clearly see Bazara puttering about as she talks excitedly on the phone.

You listen careful, your ear against the wall as you struggle to discern what this sentient vehicle is saying.

When you make out the first few words your blood runs cold.

"They're here," Baraza gushes. "They match the description perfectly."

Your heart skips a beat. You should probably tear yourself away and start running as fast as you can, but the longer you stay, the more information you'll glean.

There's also the slightest chance this conversation isn't quite what it seems, but that all goes out the window with Bazara's next sentence.

"I don't see the device yet, but they've got a bag with them," the sentient motorcycle continues. "Yes, Ted. I'll get the bag."

Suddenly, Bazara stops talking, glancing over at the window. "Hold on, I think I heard something."

Immediately, you spring into action, bounding down off the porch and running back into the junkyard as fast as you can. You begin to duck and dodge through the towers of stacked automobiles, finding your way out of this maze as you struggle to recreate the path you took on the way in.

You hear a door slam wide open and the terrifying screech of an eagle, which rings out through the yard and chills you to the bone. While you're forced to weave your way back and forth to the exit, this bird can simply fly high and swoop down to attack from above.

There's barely any time to spare.

Soon enough, you're erupting out through the main gate of the scrapyard and running down the road as fast as you can. A car full of dinosaurs is passing by and, in a moment of sheer desperation, you scream out for them to help.

A shadow swoops past overhead as the enormous bald eagle circles once, preparing to dive at you with its razor sharp talons.

"Help me!" you scream again, sprinting as fast as you can after the car full of prehistoric creatures.

Fortunately, the car slows down to a crawl and the hatchback pops open. The vehicle is almost full, but the dinosaur family is generous enough to welcome you in, cheering you on as you make a mad dash for the car.

You put all the energy you can muster into one final sprint, another horrific screech erupting above you as you leap into the back of the vehicle. "Go! Go! Go!" you scream, prompting the driver to step on the gas and blast forward.

The shadow of the eagle passes by as the car continues onward, the dinosaurs within applauding wildly.

"Thank you so much," you gush as soon as you're able to catch your breath. "You saved me."

"He is saved!" the raptors cheer excitedly.

Once you manage to collect yourself you sit up in the back and greet the other passengers. There is a mother and father dinosaur in front, and a son and daughter in the back. The far back is inhabited by you and a small cluster of road trip luggage.

These dinosaurs are conservatively dressed, and smiling so wide that it might be a little alarming if not for the fact that they've already been so kind and welcoming.

"Welcome to the Davis family road trip! I'm David Davis, this is my wife Danielle Davis and our son and daughter, Derek and Daisy Davis. Where are you headed, weary soul?" the raptor behind the wheel questions.

"San Diego," you reply.

The dinosaurs exchange excited glances, utterly blown away by this discovery.

"Hallelujah!" David Davis exclaims. "It's a miracle!"

176

"What is?" you question, a little confused.

"Every year the Davis family road trip starts in Salt Lake City," Mr. Davis begins, grinning from ear to ear. "Would you like to know where it ends up?"

"Where?" you question.

The whole car exchanges another glance, then happily announces the answer in unison. "San Diego!"

They all cheer.

"We've love to give you a ride!" David Davis continues.

"Thank you," you reply, way too exhausted to decline even if you wanted to. You sit back against the luggage, appreciating the soft bags under your weary body.

The family of raptors begins to sing along with their tape player as you settle in for a long journey.

Continue your journey on page 184

Panic washes over you as you realize this ghost is gravely sincere, and her supernatural readings are likely correct. You're not sure if you should keep listening or turn around and sprint back across the field to your truck.

"Before you go," she continues, maintaining your attention for just the slightest bit longer. "Heed these words: You must not push the button. The Big Red Button will send you to another layer or The Tingleverse, and while it will contain slightly more love than this one, this layer needs you. You must stay and protect the device. You must make your delivery and keep it from falling into the wrong hands."

"What happens if it does?" you question.

"Then it can be tampered with and reversed," the phantom explains. "It can be used to destroy the very fabric of this timeline we call home."

"I need to go then!" you cry out, the tension finally getting to you. "They're searching my truck!"

"They won't find it this time," the ghost explains. "A devil and a bigfoot are working together to steal the Big Red Button, but they won't be able to open the secret compartment. You will. Get your device and get out of there as fast as you can. Make your move when they're out searching the fields."

You stand just a moment longer, waiting to see if there's any more information to heed. The second you realize there's nothing left, you thank the ghostly woman and then take off running, sprinting out into the darkness as you make your way back toward the road.

The night air whips past you as you rush through the tall grass, but you slow down as you creep closer to your destination. A new big-rig sits parked next to your truck.

You duck into the field as two figures slowly walk out into their own headlights, talking amongst themselves as the they formulate a plan.

You can't make out their words from all the way over here, but you do manage to get a good look at the frightening characters. The first is a tall and rather imposing bigfoot, clad in a dark leather jacket and sporting an enormous beard that hangs down the front of his hairy, muscular body. He wears a patch over one eye.

The second backlit figure to emerge from the darkness is a bright red devil, a humanoid figure with stark black hair and two long, curved horns. He has a slender tail with a point at the end, which lashes around his legs as he walks. The devil is wearing a short sleeved button up shirt, and over the heart is a name tag patch that you can just barely make out. It simply reads 'Ted.'

Just like the ghost said.

From here, you can also see that the cargo hold of your truck is wide open. They've been searching for a while, doing everything they can to crack the magical code of some elusive secret compartment.

After a bit more discussion the two figures leave the road and head out into the grass, splitting off in either direction to search for the missing driver who just so happens to be watching them from the shadows.

Fortunately, neither one of the searchers is wandering in your exact direction yet, and there's plenty of ground for them to cover.

Seizing the moment, you keep your head low and rush through the grass toward the road, avoiding their line of sight as you sneak over to the cab of their truck. This vehicle, courtesy of Cobbler Trucking, has been left unlocked, and you gasp excitedly as you discover the keys have been left in the ignition. You swiftly pull out the DEVIL KEYS and put them in your pocket.

The headlights immediately shut off, which has most certainly alerted Ted and his bigfoot companion.

"Hey!" the devil cries out from the darkness in confusion.

Your eyes on the prize, you hurry back over to your own vehicle and climb into the driver's seat. Once there, you start it up with a loud roar.

As your headlights illuminate the grass before you, you see Ted with a look of absolute shock plastered over his face. He immediately points a long, clawed finger at you, attempting to cast some kind of a spell, but you're too far away and his dark magic doesn't work.

You laugh, then honk twice as you haul off down the road, literally leaving these two criminals in the dust while you continue on your way. Watching in the rearview mirror, you see them climb into their truck and then start yelling wildly, upset to discover that their keys are missing.

You drive like mad, not satisfied with pulling over until you've put as many miles between you and the other truck as possible. Even then, you make sure to turn off the main drag a bit before finding your motel for the evening.

When you finally pull into the parking lot you're absolutely exhausted, but there's still one thing left to do.

You exit the cab and head around to the back of your truck, then climb up into the cargo hold. It's completely empty, and the idea of some secret compartment hidden within these four flat, blank walls is hard to believe.

You take a deep breath and let it out, then knock three times on the wall of your truck with your hand. "Love is real," you state confidently.

Nothing happens.

Your brow furrowed, you try this process again, this time moving over to the other side of the refrigerated truck. You knock again and say the magic words, yet your results are the same.

Growing worried, you decide to give it one last go. This time, you rap your heel against the floor of the truck.

"Love is real," you say aloud.

Suddenly, there's a loud clang as a panel slides up and over, magical energy wafting up from within this tiny hidden chamber. You bend down and carefully withdraw a small box, covered in wires and sporting an enormous red button on the top. You carefully place it in your bag, then climb down from the back of the truck and close it up.

Until you reach San Diego, this bag isn't leaving your sight.

Get some rest on page 39

180

The device in that secret compartment is, as far as you can tell, one of the most important things on this timeline at the moment, and if you don't bring it with you then you might as well just surrender to Ted and his bigfoot companion right now.

You take a deep breath and let it out, centering your focus for a moment before making your move. Soon enough, you're creeping through the grass toward your truck, staying low to the ground and avoiding headlights as much as possible.

Somehow, you get to the road without the others spotting you, creeping around your truck and then climbing up into the empty cargo hold. You pull out your phone and call Truckman.

"What's up?" your boss answers almost immediately, as though he's been sitting by his phone just in case you needed help on your journey.

"I need to know the magic password," you hiss in a hushed voice, barely audible as you glance back over your shoulder.

"What?" Truckman blurts. "What's going on?"

"Cobbler Trucking just showed up and ransacked the shipment," you explain.

"The milk doesn't matter. Did they find the machine?" your boss immediately demands to know.

"No," you whisper. "They're out looking for me. I need to get the device and get out of here before they come back. I'm in the back of the truck now."

Your boss realizes how tense your current situation truly is, springing into action and focusing on the task at hand.

"Knock three times on the floor, then say the words 'love is real'", Truckman instructs. "That's how you open the secret compartment."

You rap your heel against the ground three times. "Love is real," you say under your breath.

There's a loud clang as a panel slides up and over, magical energy wafting from within this tiny hidden chamber. The sounds make you tense up for minute, listening hard to see if Ted or the bigfoot noticed, but there's no sign they're making their way back to the truck just yet.

You bend down and carefully withdraw a small box, covered in wires and sporting an enormous red button on the top. You carefully place it in your bag, then close the magic compartment and climb down from the back of the cargo hold.

"I've got the device," you inform your boss.

"What you're holding is The Big Red Button," Truckman explains. "Anyone who presses it will transport into a timeline with slightly more love, which is great, but *you* can't press it just yet. We need you here in this reality to protect the device. You've gotta get it to San Diego before it has a chance to fall into the wrong hands. If Ted Cobbler reverse engineers that machine, he could destroy the very fabric of this timeline."

"I've got this," you reply, sneaking off into the darkness and hurrying down the road.

"Get out of there," Truckman continues. "Leave your truck, just make the delivery. It doesn't matter how."

"Okay," you reply.

"And don't fly!" he suddenly cries out. "The Big Red Button can't handle the pressure."

"Understood," you confirm, then hang up the phone.

With no other option available, you continue onward into the darkness. You're jogging for the first hour or so, but eventually you tire and start walking.

You're ready to jump off the road and hide in the tall grass at any sign of a big-rig rumbling after you, but that never happens. They're likely still trying to get the compartment open, not realizing the device within is already gone.

As you continue on your way, your eyes begin to adjust to the darkness even more, the wide open plains opening up to you in every direction. The stars above seem even more brilliant than before, and for a while you actually get to appreciate the stillness and beauty of it all. Sure, you're on an important mission, but right now it feels like the only thing that matters is the glorious size of the universe that hangs above you.

You walk all night, and the entire time not a single car comes down this road to pass you by. As the dawn breaks, however, a modest yellow sedan comes puttering along from behind. Eventually, the car pulls over next to you, the rising sun casting the driver's face with a beautiful golden glow as they roll down their window.

A sentient corn on the cob sits in the vehicle before you, her body partially wrapped in a green leafy shell while the rest features several rows of yellow kernels.

"Need a ride?" the sentient corn asks.

182

You immediately pick up on good vibes from this living vegetable, but you also remember that you can never be too sure on a mission like this.

"Where are you headed?" you question.

"Started in Nebraska, driving down to Vegas," she explains.

That covers most of the distance between here and San Diego, you immediately realize.

Accept the ride on page 161
Decline on page 68

"Okay," you reply with a smile, not sure when you'll have another opportunity to share a dance with someone from beyond the grave.

You take the ghostly woman's hand in yours and soon enough the two of you have joined the other sprits, dancing and frolicking right there in the middle of Home of Truth's tiny town square. The other phantoms welcome you gladly, and it's not long before you've completely forgotten their otherworldly nature.

The band kicks into high gear, segueing into one song after another as you twist and twirl the night away. They clap their hands and stomp their feet, jovially shouting out words of encouragement to their new friend.

Even after the dancing has finished, you stick around a while to chat with the citizens of this ghostly hamlet, trading stories as you offer up tales from the road.

It's a wonderful time, but as the night wears on you eventually realize that you've gotta pull yourself away.

When you inform the ghosts it's your time to go they all boo loudly, then accept this reality and offer you a series of kind goodbyes.

The last to see you off is the ghostly woman who you first danced with, a spirit you now know as Remla.

"Have a good trip," the phantom offers warmly. "I know I told you the timelines of the dead and the living shouldn't cross, but you're just so kind. I'd like to offer up a little more advice."

"Are you sure that's alright?" you question.

Remla shrugs. "Who knows? What I *do* know is that a rival truck company, Cobbler Trucking, is searching your truck right now."

"Wait... what?" you blurt.

Remla nods. "They're looking for something called The Big Red Button, which is in a secret compartment. You have to knock three times and say 'love is real' to open it."

You can't help but laugh. "You're joking right?"

Remla shakes her head.

As wonderful as your night has been thus far, you're still not sure if you trust this strange apparition. For all you know, she could just be trying to scare you again.

Trust her on page 177
Disbelieve on page 144

184

Over the rest of the journey you become incredibly friendly with the Davis family, the raptors welcoming you in with open arms and making sure you feel like an important part of their yearly road trip. All this despite the fact that you're just some random stranger they happened to pick up on the way, but that just goes to show how kind and considerate these dinosaurs really are.

By the time you reach San Diego, it feels like you're all best friends.

It's late in the afternoon by the time their sedan pulls up to the wharf, packed full of luggage and love. The sunset blossoms over the ocean behind you, and a giant warehouse with the address you've been looking for sits only a few yards away, now right within your grasp.

You give David Davis a warm hug, thanking him profusely for his hospitality out on the road.

"It was our pleasure," the raptor offers, then turns to his family as they wait in the car behind him.

"That's right!" Danielle Davis chimes in.

"Have a good delivery!" Derek Davis calls out from the back seat. "Hope that devil doesn't find you!"

You wave as David climbs back into the driver's seat and then circles around, heading back up the hill and away from the wharf.

Soon enough, you're all alone. The only sounds now are the soft lapping of waves against the shore and the distant call of a lone seagull.

You look down at your phone, reminding yourself of the scientist that you're looking for. Truckman has sent you a photograph, and you read the name below it aloud to yourself.

"Borson Reems," you say, taking in this middle-aged man's enormous white beard and round nose. He has a kindness in his expression that is truly something to behold.

Your bag gripped tight, you walk toward the enormous oceanside warehouse, strolling up to the door and pushing it open.

"Hello?" you call out, your voice echoing across the cavernous space of this wide open industrial building. The ceilings are high and the floor is all cement, giving the space a very specific sonic texture.

There's no response, so you creep in a little more.

"Borson?" you call out, gazing up at the birds perched on a high metal beam above you.

"Yes!" comes a jovial voice from around the corner.

Soon enough, Borson Reems is stepping into view. He's a short, stout man with brilliant blue eyes and red cheeks. While he's currently working as a scientist, you've heard from Truckman that he spends most of his time out on the water as a fisherman.

The two of you step toward one another, Borson Reaching out toward you in an attempt to take the bag, but suddenly you stop in your tracks.

There was a distinct kindness and soul that was apparent in your photo of Borson, but now that he's standing before you, that inner light seems to be missing for some reason. You feel incredibly silly about your hesitation, but you just can't help yourself.

"Are you alright?" Borson Reems questions.

"Yeah, I'm fine," you stammer, struggling to parse the unexpected feeling of danger that has suddenly overwhelmed your senses.

You shake your head, rattling your mind back into alignment. This has been a long, harrowing journey, so it's no wonder the promise of a peaceful resolution has made you skeptical.

However, now that you've made it to the end, you shouldn't talk yourself out of crossing the finish line. You don't want to be your own worst enemy.

"Do you have the button?" Borson questions.

You nod.

"Then hand it over!" he cries out, growing frustrated. "There's not much time! Ted Cobbler could be here any minute"

Hand over The Big Red Button on page 139
Hesitate on page 167

The plan was always to retire, but as your adventure on that fateful day made very clear, things don't always go according to plan.

With your new business partner, Keith the billionaire jet plane, you were able to pour enough money into Truckman Trucking that it became and international shipping company, spanning a variety of different vehicle types. Your boss was so impressed with your hard work, in fact, that he made you and Keith the joint heads of the company once he stepped down.

Of course, Ted Cobbler was there every step of the way trying to stop you with some evil plan, but evil plans will only ever get you so far in this world. With love on your side, and a firm desire to get products where they're going, Truckman Trucking eventually put Cobbler Enterprises out of business for good.

"Where are you going?" Keith calls out to you from his corner office.

You're strolling by, heading toward the elevators when he notices your escape.

"Making a trip," you reply. "I'll be back on Monday."

The sentient jet plane just shakes his head in both confusion and reverence. "I can't believe you're still doing that," he offers. "You know you're the boss, right?"

You shrug. "I'm the boss, which means if I wanna drive a shipment of spaghetti to Florida over the weekend, then that's exactly what I'll do."

Keith laughs, still not getting it but appreciating your desires all the same. "Alright, alright. I'll see you on Monday."

You continue to the elevator and step inside, pressing a button for the shipping warehouse. Your truck is already loaded up and waiting for you, and you can't wait to get behind the wheel.

THE END

You suddenly remember the pack of BUBBLEGUM that's been sitting in your pocket since Idaho. You reach in and pull it out as quietly as you can, then pop a stick into your mouth. You chew quickly and softly, struggling to walk the line but making it work and, eventually, ending up with a small piece of malleable gum the approximate size of the hole you've been staring through.

You can see that the enormous eagle has started to peck around the area, gradually moving closer and closer to your hiding spot in the rusty barrel, but you don't wait around to see what happens next. Instead, you push your gum into the tiny hole, plunging the barrel into complete darkness but fully blocking you from view.

You hold your breath and patiently wait, growing alarmed when you hear the bald eagle brushing up against the side of your metal drum, then flooded with relief when the predator continues onward. Soon enough, you hear another frightening screech from the bird, only this time it's emitting from off in the distance, the creature taking flight once again and performing its search elsewhere.

Now is your chance.

You quietly lift up the edge of the oil barrel and crawl out from under it, climbing to your feet and then running back the way you came. You wind your way through the maze a bit longer, but eventually find yourself emerging onto the road.

You don't hesitate, kicking into high gear as you sprint back to the motel as fast as your legs can carry you. When you arrive, you pull out your newly pilfered tin of *MAGIC BOOT CREAM*, scooping out a huge glob of the strange, shimmering substance and then wiping it all over the boot that's been attached to your front wheel.

The goop sizzles with a swirling magical energy, emitting a strange hiss as it works its magic. You watch in amazement as the powerful compounds begin to react, and moments later the automotive boot emits a loud clang as it splits open and releases your truck from its metallic grasp.

No time to waste, you throw open the door of your cab and climb in, then start up your trusty big-rig with a deafening roar. As you pull out onto the road once again, you find yourself unable to stop smiling, blown away by the adventure that your final ride has unexpectedly become.

Keep on truckin' to page 93

You decide to stay and face these bullies head on, but as the truck stops and the doors open you wonder if that was such a good idea. You're trying to maintain a confident outlook, but deep down you're absolutely terrified.

From out of the darkness two silhouettes emerge, one much larger than the other. The enormous figure soon reveals himself to be a rather imposing bigfoot, clad in a dark leather jacket and sporting an enormous beard that hangs down the front of his hairy, muscular body. He has a patch over one eye.

The bigfoot reveals himself and then stops, hanging back as his partner steps forward.

The second backlit form to emerge from the darkness is a bright red devil, a humanoid figure with stark black hair and two long, curved horns. He has a slender tail with a point at the end, which lashes around his legs as he walks. The devil is wearing a short sleeved button up shirt, and over the heart is a small name tag patch that simply reads 'Ted.'

"Hand over the device," Ted demands, the devils voice drifting across your ears with a deep and menacing tone.

"I have no idea what you're talking about," you reply.

"Go around and look in the back," Ted commands the bigfoot. "I guess our friend won't mind us taking a look around."

As the bigfoot follows Ted's orders you rush to stop him. The second you move, however, the devil reaches out toward you with his clawed red hand. Suddenly, a magical eruption of searing pain overwhelms your body, causing you to cry out loud as you collapse to your knees in agony.

"I wouldn't do that," Ted offers with a gleeful smile, twisting his hand as he continues to pump magical pain waves into your nervous system.

When you've finally had enough, Ted relents, causing you to crumble into an exhausted heap.

Meanwhile, the muscular bigfoot has arrived at the back of your truck and picked up a large rock from the side of the road. He approaches the cargo hold lock and begins to hammer away at it, slamming his boulder across the metal over and over again until finally it pops open and falls into the gravel with a thud.

The bigfoot throws open the roll up door, then climbs up into the refrigerated shipping container. The next thing you know, your ears are assaulted by the sound of hundreds of chocolate milk crates being opened up and smashed onto the asphalt road below. The bigfoot is ruthless, tearing through the contents of your truck as you watch in absolute horror.

Ted may have powerful magic at his disposal, but maybe you can fight your way through the pain and somehow stop this bigfoot from destroying your entire shipment.

Stop him on page 114
Stay calm and wait on page 112

190

Something catches your eye, the front end of Ted's enormous black and red big-rig truck poking out from around the other side of the warehouse. It's intentionally obscured from view, as it would've given away the devil's little trick, but clearly not hidden well enough.

You reach into your pocket, your fingers tracing along the edge of the devil truck key that's hidden within as inspiration begins to flood your senses. You have a very, very crazy idea, but that crazy edge is exactly why it just might work.

Springing into action, you sprint over to the enormous truck, climbing up into the cab and starting it with a loud roar. The giant machine begins to purr as you pull it back a bit, allowing yourself a little runway. It's even more powerful and massive than the vehicle you're used to, which is definitely saying something.

You have one last chance to reconsider whether or not this is a good idea, but that's a chance you don't take. Instead, you slam your foot onto the gas pedal and rumble toward the wall of the warehouse, aiming for the approximate location where Ted and his one-eyed bigfoot companion had been standing within.

The vehicle picks up speed and soon enough it's smashing through the wall, stone and metal cascading everywhere. The truck rolls to an abrupt stop as dust hangs in the air, obscuring your vision as you struggle to get a read on the fallout of this incredibly reckless maneuver.

You open the door, climbing down into the haze as you search for answers. Moments later, a silhouetted figure stumbles toward you through the dust, coughing loudly as they struggle to collect themselves.

It's Borson Reems.

"You're alive!" you cry out.

Borson smiles. "I suppose I am."

"Where are they?" you continue, eyes peeled as you wait for the diabolical villains to make their return.

The scientist points down at the rubble beneath your feet. "I don't think they're going anywhere for a while."

You stare out across the San Diego shoreline from the deck of your oceanside hotel, enjoying the beach and the glorious sunset beyond. It's your first night of retirement, and you couldn't be happier. You were hoping for an exciting last ride, after all, and that one certainly fits the bill.

You reach over and grab the glass of ice cold chocolate milk sitting next to you, taking a long, satisfying pull from the sweet and delicious beverage.

This is what it's all about.

As the sounds of the ocean hums peacefully in your ears, you kick up your feet and pull out your phone, hoping to read a little bit of the local news.

You smile when you see the first headline, reading it aloud to yourself. "Evil plan underperforms: Ted Cobbler and bigfoot companion thwarted at the wharf."

THE END

A long black limousine suddenly pulls up next to you, rolling along at the same speed that you're running. The door pops open, offering an escape that you gladly accept. Without a second thought you dive into the vehicle, watching as the unicorns slow and eventually stop, the angry gang fading into the distance.

You let out a sigh of relief, but this moment is short lived.

"Looks like it's your lucky day," comes a familiar voice.

You turn to see Ted sitting across from you, the bright red devil smiling wide from his comfortable seat in the back of the limo. You immediately try tearing open the door next to you and escaping out onto the street, but the doors refuse to open.

"You won't get out," Ted offers with a laugh. "My friend Bazara, the lock wizard, had magical locks installed. Only I can open them."

With no place left to run, you consider lunging at Ted, but before you get a chance the devil reaches out with a clawed hand and sends a blast of pain waves through your body.

You cry out in agony, every nerve sizzling in unison as you curl up into a ball. You drop your bag to the ground, and with his other hand Ted reaches over and snatches it up.

"Got it!" you hear the devil call out, prompting the limo driver to slow down and pull over to the curb.

Still flooding your form with excruciating pain, Ted climbs past you and opens up the door. He steps out onto the street and extracts The Big Red Button from your bag, then waves it in the air at you.

"Thanks for the present," Ted offers with a devilish grin. He slams the door shut and raps twice on the top of the vehicle.

To your great relief, the pain immediately stops, but with The Big Red Button no longer in your possession there's not much to celebrate. You immediately start kicking against the window of the limo. Unfortunately, the magical reinforcements are simply too powerful, and you just end up hurting your foot.

The partition rolls down between you and your driver.

"That's not gonna work," they inform you. "You can't get up here either."

You reach out to test this theory, extending your hand and watching as a blue magical light erupts across the space between these two sections of the vehicle. There's some sort of force field.

"Where are we going?" you question.

The driver shrugs. "Doesn't matter. I thought we could drive out into the desert for a good show."

"What are you talking about?" you ask. "Why doesn't it matter?"

"It's the end of the world," the driver continues. "I just figured you might wanna watch from somewhere nice."

You fall back against your seat now, realizing there's no way out of this. Ted has The Big Red Button and it's only a matter of time before he reverse engineers the device. Soon enough, he'll be tearing this reality apart.

Through the windows of the limousine you watches as the lights of the city fade away, welcomed into the wide open desert on some dusty back road. The stars shimmer brilliantly in the sky above you, and the driver rolls open the sunroof so you can get a better look. Of course, he informs you there's a force field up there, too.

You just stare in wonder at the vast beauty of space above. An hour or two goes by before your start to notice any changes, but soon enough the stars are moving, melting and twisting into one another as they dissolve into nothing. You watch in a mixture of horror and amazement as reality begins to break apart, returning to a mess of primordial atoms.

THE END

You decide to stay and face these bullies head on, but as the truck stops and the doors open you begin to wonder if that was such a good idea. You're trying to maintain a confident outlook, but deep down you're absolutely terrified.

From out of the darkness two silhouettes emerge, one much larger than the other. The enormous figure soon reveals himself to be a rather imposing bigfoot, clad in a dark leather jacket and sporting an enormous beard that hangs down the front of his hairy, muscular body. He's wearing a patch over one eye.

The bigfoot reveals himself and then stops, hanging back as his partner steps forward.

The second backlit form to emerge from the darkness is a bright red devil, a humanoid figure with stark black hair and two long, curved horns. He has a slender tail with a point at the end, which lashes around his legs as he walks. The devil is wearing a short sleeved button up shirt, and over the heart is a small name tag patch that simply reads 'Ted.'

"Hand over the device," Ted demands, the devils voice drifting across your ears with a deep and menacing tone.

"I have no idea what you're talking about," you reply.

Ted narrows his eyes and the bigfoot takes an aggressive step toward you, but the devil suddenly throws up his hand to stop his friend's approach.

"Go around and look in the back," Ted commands the bigfoot. "I guess our friend won't mind us taking a look around."

"I was robbed," you blurt.

"We'll see about that," Ted counters with a doubtful smirk.

Ted's companion does as he's told, walking around to the back of your truck and then picking up a large rock from the side of the road. He approaches the lock and begins to hammer away at it, slamming his boulder across the metal over and over again until finally it pops open and falls into the gravel with a thud.

The bigfoot throws open the roll up door, then calls out to Ted. "There's nothing back here," he yells. "The truck is empty."

The devil's grin falters slightly. Clearly he wasn't expecting this.

"What?" Ted blurts.

You decide that now might be a good time to interject again. "I told you, I was robbed," you repeat. "A bunch of jackalopes got in the back when I was headed through Wyoming."

Ted's eyes go wide as you say this. The bigfoot comes back around to meet him and, without a word, the two of them turn and march back over to their enormous red and black truck. They climb in, slamming the doors and pulling out onto the road once again.

They roar off into the night.

You stand in silence for a moment, still reeling from what just happened, then immediately spring into action as you pull out your *SPARE TRUCK TIRE* and get to work.

It's not long before you've replaced the flat. You take a moment, wiping the sweat from your brow, then climb back up into your cab and hit the road.

You call Truckman.

"It's late!" your boss blurts as he answers the phone. "Is everything okay?"

"No," you reply. "Definitely not okay. I just got accosted by a devil and his bigfoot henchman. They're working for Cobbler Trucking."

"Ted," your boss replies matter of factly. "Ted Cobbler."

"That's the one," you offer. "They asked me where the device was and I said I didn't know. I told them some jackalopes robbed me up north."

"And they left?" Truckman continues.

"They did," you reply.

Your boss breathes an audible sigh of relief, but the moment doesn't last long. "You need to get out of there," Truckman informs you. "Once they realize the jackalopes don't have it, they'll come back searching and they'll come back angry."

"What's the device?" you demand, sick of all the secrets.

Truckman sighs loudly. "I suppose I can tell you now that it's come to this. What you have in your truck is something called The Big Red Button. Every timeline has one, and although they exist in a variety of different forms and shapes, they all serve the same purpose. Anyone who pushes The Big Red Button will descend deeper into The Tingleverse, traveling downward through the layers of reality."

"I'm... not entirely sure what that means," you admit.

"That's fine," Truckman explains. "Just don't push the button, and don't let if fall into the wrong hands."

"Why not push the button?" you question. "What if the next

timeline is better?"

"It *is* better, but that's exactly why you can't leave this one. You're here to protect the button at all costs, and if you leave this timeline they'll be nobody here to look after it," your boss explains. "If a scoundrel finds The Big Red Button they could easily reverse engineer it and create a device that brings negative timelines into this one, making the universe progressively more terrible. They could even program the button to tear this reality apart."

"I've got this," you reply confidently. "You can count on me to get this delivery where it needs to go."

"I know, that's why I selected you for this trip," Truckman explains. "Now that you know what's back there, you should keep The Big Red Button on you at all times. Take it out of the back and put it in your bag."

"I would if I could," you counter. "I don't know how to get into the secret compartment."

"Just go into the cargo hold and knock on the floor of the container three times, then say the words 'love is real.'"

"Got it," you reply.

You drive a while longer before finally pulling off at a motel in the middle of nowhere, the first place you spot with a flickering vacancy sign. You climb into the back of your truck and follow Truckman's instructions, rapping three times on the floor with the heel of your shoe and then announcing the magic words.

Immediately, a sliding door opens up to reveal a small mechanical device hidden just beneath the surface of this refrigerated chamber. It's rectangular and covered in wires, featuring an enormous red circle on one side of the box. You pull it out and carefully place it into your bag.

Wasting no time, you check in and then retire to your room for the evening, The Big Red Button sitting safe and sound by your side.

Get some rest on page 39

After considering your options you decide that the best thing to do is wait. Right now, there's just not enough information to work with, and you'd hate to risk tipping this bucket just to find that you're slithering at Ted's feet.

You listen in a bit more, hearing this new voice start to chant and work though some strange incantation. As they mumble words to themselves, more voices join the mix, strange disembodied tones that fill the air with bizarre vocalizations. Various phrases pop in and out of the mix, syllables disconnected and then reconnected like a thousand conversations in a crowded room. It's fascinating to listen to, but moments later it abruptly stops.

"Love is... something," the voice offers. "We're almost there."

"Wonderful!" Ted exclaims.

"I need five minutes to collect myself," the new voice continues, "this ritual takes a lot of out of you. We'll have it cracked soon enough."

There's a brief pause. "I've got just the thing to kill some time," Ted suddenly announces.

You hear footsteps and feel their vibrations through the floor below you, growing closer and closer until, suddenly, the top is whipped off of your bucket.

The bright red devil reaches inside and grabs you firmly with his long claws, lifting you up and looking you right in the eye. "We don't need your help anymore," he states bluntly. "The password is almost ours."

You can see now that you're in some kind of shack. It's covered in American flags and patriotic paraphernalia, and next to Ted is, in fact, a sentient motorcycle with long dark hair.

The most terrifying thing, however, is an enormous cage in the corner with a giant eagle held within. The second this giant bird sees you it begins to shriek and squawk, biting the bars with its razor sharp beak and slashing them with its talons.

Ted smiles menacingly, then carries you over to the eagle.

"You think he's hungry?" Ted asks mischievously.

"Always," the motorcycle replies.

You try your best to squirm away but it's no use. Ted pops open a latch on the cage, then tosses you inside.

You immediately try to slither away but the eagle is just too fast, lunging down and snatching you up in its beak. You feel a sharp, searing

198

pain across your back as darkness envelopes you, torn in half and sliding down the throat of the giant eagle.

THE END

You decide to take your chances.

Cautiously, you begin to creep deeper into the structure, your eyes scanning the warehouse for any signs of a still functioning timeline tear.

Your heart begins to slam hard within your chest, not from the thought that you'll be traveling to some other reality, but out of the fear that you might never get a chance. If the explosion caused a clean break in timelines, there might not even be a portal to slip through.

You take one more step and then suddenly find yourself tumbling forward, falling through the floor as you spiral through a tunnel that rests far outside your basic understanding of space and time. The world around you is stretching and contorting, carrying you through a cascade of potential realities like a book with multiple paths and endings.

You find yourself broken down into the most basic version of yourself, *ANY ITEMS* that you're carrying disappearing into the either as though they never existed in the first place. Along with these objects go your memories, the journey you just experienced fading away as your mind is born anew.

You gasp suddenly, as though waking from an exceptionally vivid daydream. You've found yourself sanding outside Truckman's office, but you're not exactly sure how you got there.

It takes a moment for the thoughts to collect themselves within your head, but soon enough it all begins creeping back.

Enter Truckman's office on page 1

You begin to rock the bucket back and forth, slithering hard to one side and then the other in a rhythmic motion. At first it seems like your attempts are going nowhere, but as you start to build momentum you realize the container is actually tilting.

Soon enough, the bucket falls to the ground and the wooden board on top of it slides off. You immediately freeze, worried this noise is going to draw the attention of your captors, but it seems their back room discussion is loud enough to cover for you.

Quietly, you slither out onto the floor, finding yourself in a wooden shack of some kind. It's hard to get a feel for the place when your body sits so low to the ground, but from what you can tell you're in a storage room. The voices continue from somewhere out front, a cracked open door all that separates the two of you.

As you gaze through the sliver of an opening, you also catch a glimpse of an enormous bald eagle in a cage, the creature walking back and forth on its perch while it listens intently to the heated conversation before it.

You duck away, then crawl in the other direction as you struggle to avoid this massive bird's line of sight.

Making your way along the bottom of several shelves, you notice an assortment of potions and tinctures. Whoever owns this place is a dark wizard of some kind, with a specific bent toward magic locks and seals.

Suddenly, one of the containers catches your eye. There's a picture on the label of a snake transforming into a human, a message that couldn't be more clear and immediately sends a surge of adrenaline rushing through your cold-blooded body.

You bite into the cork with your sharp snake teeth, gripping tight and then popping it off. With this hard jerk you accidently knock the potion over, spilling it everywhere, but you don't mind. You begin to frantically lap up the strange, swirling liquid, using your forked tongue to taste the magical concoction.

A sharp jolt of pain suddenly rips through your body, but you refuse to cry out in alarm. Instead, you bite your lip, allowing your bones to lengthen and your skin to soften as you make the magical transformation between reptile and mammal.

Soon enough, you've regained your previous form, appearing exactly how you started.

Unfortunately, you don't have much time to celebrate. You immediately head to the nearby window and ever so slightly crack it open, lifting up the pane just far enough so that you can slip out.

You now find yourself standing outside on a brisk afternoon, surrounded by piles of junky cars and twisted metal. You're in a scrapyard, dropped into the center of an enormous maze with no clues to help you escape.

That is, of course, until you notice the two familiar trucks parked right next to you. On one side is Ted's red and black vehicle, and on the other is your trusty big-rig.

Driven by some potent force of survival, you immediately creep over the Ted's truck and climb up into the cab. The DEVIL KEYS have been left inside, so you pull them out of the ignition and take them for yourself. This should keep Ted from chasing after you, at least for a little while.

You climb back down and then hurry over to the rig of your own, opening up the door and climbing into the driver's seat with a wide smile plastered across your face. This pilot's chair might not be much, but right now it's a sight for sore eyes.

You take a deep breath, enjoying a brief moment of silence before the chaos begins, then start your truck.

The vehicle roars to life and you throw it into drive, peeling out into the maze of stacked metal and deftly weaving through the towers. Ted, the one-eyed bigfoot and a sentient motorcycle with long dark hair all burst out of the shack to watch you roll away.

"Get him!" Ted cries.

The bigfoot sprints over to their red and black truck and hops inside.

"Go!" screams Ted, growing more and more frustrated by the second while the bigfoot refuses to act.

Moments later the bigfoot cracks open his door. "The keys are gone!" he exclaims.

By now, you're already pulling out onto the open road, getting the hell out of there and driving South as far and as fast as possible.

You continue like this for hours, the surge of adrenalin that courses through your freshly human body taking forever to finally dissipate. Once it does, you pull into a rest area and call Truckman.

"Hello?" your boss offers, picking up his phone on the first ring.

"Yeah, I just got turned into a snake," you blurt, clearly upset. "A damn snake! A no arms, no legs, forked tongue slithering snake!"

"Whoa, whoa, whoa," Truckman blurts. "Slow down. What happened?"

"A literal devil and a one-eyed bigfoot turned me into a snake, then they stole the truck and I stole it back. They were trying to find the device, but they couldn't figure out how to open up the secret compartment. They took the truck to a lock wizard, but that's when I escaped."

"So they *didn't* get the device?" Truckman clarifies, cutting right to the chase.

"Nope," you reply proudly.

Your boss breaths and audible sigh of relief. "I guess it's time I told you what's going on," he begins. "You're carrying something called The Big Red Button. When this button is pushed it will send you to a new layer of reality with slightly more love and this one. It's a powerful tool, but there are devils, like Ted Cobbler, who would like to reverse engineer The Big Red Button and create something that could tear this timeline apart. You've gotta get the device to San Diego, and can't let it fall into the wrong hands."

"So far so good," you reply.

"I guess it's a matter of perspective on that one," Truckman retorts. "From now on, keep The Big Red Button close. I'll help you open the secret compartment to fetch it."

"And how do I do that?" you ask.

"Knock three times and say 'love is real'", your boss explains. "Simple as that."

"Got it," you reply. "Thanks."

You hang up the phone, then exit your cab. You head around to the back of the truck, hoisting yourself up into the cargo hold. It's completely empty, and the idea of some secret compartment hidden within these four flat, blank walls is hard to believe.

You take a deep breath and let it out, then knock three times on the wall of your truck with your hand. "Love is real," you state confidently.

Nothing happens.

Your brow furrowed, you try this process again, this time moving over to the other side of the refrigerated truck. You knock again and say the magic words, yet your results are the same.

Growing worried, you decide to give it one last go. This time, you rap your heel against the floor of the truck.

"Love is real," you say aloud.

Suddenly, there's a loud clang as a panel slides over, magical energy wafting up from within this tiny hidden chamber. You bend down and carefully withdraw a small box, covered in wires and sporting an enormous red button on the top. You carefully place it in your bag, then climb down from the back of the truck and close it up.

With a renewed sense of purpose you return to the driver's seat and pull back out onto the road.

You keep driving and you don't look back.

Roll on to page 93

There's suddenly an enormous eruption behind you, the earsplitting boom momentarily deafening your senses and sending a shock wave through your body. You turn to witness the whole warehouse splitting apart in a ball of brilliant blue energy, an explosion unlike anything you've ever seen.

Stranger still, this eruption slows to a stop almost instantly, the shattered warehouse scraps hanging briefly in the air before suddenly pulling back together and contracting into the exact same position they once occupied.

As the crackling energy dissipates you sprint back toward the warehouse, rushing inside to find that everyone has disappeared.

You suddenly realize that Borson Reems had been lying. He couldn't actually determine a way to stabilize The Big Red Button, but that didn't matter when all you're trying to do is transport someone off of this reality and onto another.

Borson sacrificed himself to send Ted and the one-eyed bigfoot to some other random timeline where they can't get their hands on The Big Red Button... but neither can he.

Feeling overwhelmed with emotion, you pull out your phone and call Truckman.

"What happened?" he immediately questions after picking up.

"They're gone," you blurt.

"What?" your boss replies. "Who is?"

"Borson, Ted," you stammer. "There was so much chaos, it's hard to say. I think Borson created an explosion that destroyed The Big Red Button and sent them all to another timeline.

Truckman lets out a long sigh, finally understanding. "You tried your best," he tells you. "The delivery was made and that's all you can really hope for. Borson may be gone, but *this* timeline is still intact."

"I guess you're right," you say, begrudgingly accepting his kind words.

"You should be proud," your boss reassures you. "Take a day off by the beach then head back up to Billings. Try and enjoy the trip this time."

"That sounds pretty good," you admit.

"Just don't stick around there for too long," Truckman continues. "Those timeline explosions are unstable. The rift will likely stay torn for a while and you don't wanna accidently slip through."

"Sure thing," you reply, then hang up the phone.

You stand here in the middle of the warehouse for a moment, knowing what happens next but somehow unable to get started. You find yourself feeling strangely conflicted.

This isn't a terrible ending to your final ride, but it's certainly bittersweet. You can't help feeling like you might be able to travel back through the rift and do things a little differently next time.

Of course, who knows where the timeline tear will send you, but it might be worth a shot if that means a better ending for Borson Reems.

Search for the timeline rift on page 199
Accept this journey and head to the hotel on page 154

Printed in Great Britain
by Amazon

35237000R00119